A FII

Back to 1890.

A FIFTH FORM MARTYR

E M Channon
(MRS FRANCIS CHANNON)

.

Books to Treasure

Books to Treasure
5 Woodview Terrace,
Nailsea, Bristol, BS48 1AT
UK

www.bookstotreasure.co.uk

First published by Sheldon Press 1935
This edition 2015

Design and layout © Books to Treasure

ISBN 978-1-909423-25-1

TO

MARGARET EYRE

SHE KNOWS WHY

CONTENTS

PREFACE

E M Channon was born Ethel Mary Bredin on 17 October 1875 in Ireland. After her father's death four years later, she and her mother moved to St Leonard's where she attended the Ladies' College. She married Rev Francis Channon in 1904 and together they had six children. Ethel began writing after her marriage and produced numerous books for both children and adults. She is, perhaps, best known for *The Honour of the House*, which was published in 1931, but she wrote another dozen or so stories for girls between 1924 and 1937. She died on 6 June 1941.

PUBLISHER'S NOTE

As can be seen from the image below, the dustwrapper on the first edition was plain text on an undecorated sheet of (pink) paper, rather than illustrated as we have come to expect. The frontispiece, however, was produced in colour, and we have taken the liberty of using the frontispiece to create an illustrated cover for this Books to Treasure edition. Both internal text and the book's boards list the title as *A Fifth Form Martyr*, so that's what we have done on our cover rather than following the shortened form of the original dustwrapper..

Adrianne Fitzpatrick

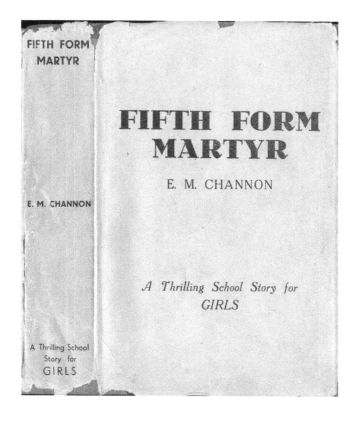

A FIFTH FORM MARTYR

CHAPTER I

JOAN GROUSE

THE Fifth were discussing their coming holidays—not so very near, unfortunately, for it was still not quite half-term. But Peggy Mills had such amazing prospects—she was actually going, of all places, to Constantinople—that she simply couldn't keep them to herself for a minute; and when other people had expressed the proper amount of amazement and envy and interest, they had of course to give some account of their own much milder expectations. Stella Purves was going to Scotland. Anne Temple was going to Brittany. Alison Hughes, needless to say, hadn't any idea of what she was going to do; but that was quite the natural thing in an artistic family, where plans were made and scrapped at two minutes' notice, and nobody ever knew the day of the month, or which tennis-racket belonged to whom. Philippa Minchin was just describing, in her careful, precious way that was so exceptionally irritating, the exact stage of her mother's arrangements about going to Buxton and how tiresome the hotel people were, and everyone was thinking of something else and yet patiently trying to be polite, when Audrey Bute (who didn't know the meaning of either patience or politeness) suddenly looked in another direction and exclaimed:

"Hullo! Here's Joan Grouse!"

It was Audrey who had given her that name; and the name had stuck like glue. Joan Partridge herself hated it passionately for the best of all good reasons, because it was too true. She

was a confirmed grouser: she *did* behave like Mrs. Gummidge,
believing that everything unpleasant that happened was worse
for her than for anybody else: and, if she went about looking
like a martyr three days out of four, she was most thoroughly
convinced that she had every justification for doing so.

"Hullo, Joan!" said one and another courteous person, with
an unnatural heartiness. "Heard Peggy's news?"

Joan said, in words, only: "No, I haven't." But her tone and
her manner and her expression all said for her, as plainly as
possible, that she didn't want to hear it, and wasn't interested,
and didn't mean to pretend that she was.

"She's going to Constantinople!"

"*Is* she?" said Joan, impressed in spite of herself. But, again,
everything about her conveyed an instant distinct further
impression that it was only what she would have expected—
that sort of fabulous holiday naturally occurred to everyone
in the world, except the unfortunate Joan Partridge. In the
face of it, even Peggy (who was of course bubbling over with
excitement and enthusiasm) couldn't dilate on her own good
luck. She was a kind girl. With an immense effort, she switched
off from her own prospects, and inquired instead what Joan
herself was going to do.

"We always do the same thing. We go to my grandfather in
Shropshire."

"That's rather a jolly part, isn't it?" Peggy persisted nobly.

"Oh, yes! Quite."

The voice was so damping that even Peggy, that soul of
good-nature, retired hurt. Audrey, a very different person,
hurled herself into the fray. Had the grandfather a nice house?
Yes: quite nice. Garden, and so on? Well, yes: a park, if you
came to that. Yes, and two cars: yes, and horses: yes, and a hard
tennis-court and two grass ones. Did Joan ride, and get plenty
of tennis, and were the people round friendly and jolly? Oh,
yes: quite.

"Well, you really are the most ungrateful of all lucky blighters, Joan Grouse!" said Audrey pungently; and the general silence of other people supplied an affirmative chorus.

Joan looked round in her lack-lustre way. Meeting, as she was accustomed to meet, disapproving glances in every direction, she was moved to a languid self-defence.

"We go there *every* year. It gets rather boring."

"Perhaps you'd rather come to seaside lodgings with us?" Audrey flung at her. "Eight of us—five bedrooms, smallish—one big sitting-room for the whole lot!"

Joan looked at her silently, in an incredulous dismay. Her glance said so plainly what she was thinking, that Audrey answered it stridently.

"You think that awful, don't you? You didn't know that any decent people lived that way? Well, we do! and we have a most ripping time! We go every year to a little Welsh place, and swim, and boat, and play cricket on the sands with the boys, and we wouldn't do anything else for—for anything!"

The air was becoming so electric, that perhaps it was just as well that a diversion occurred at that heated moment. No one had noticed the parlour-maid's entrance; but there she was, waiting patiently for a pause in Audrey's remarks, so that she might give her message.

"Will Miss Partridge go to the drawing-room, please?"

"Now, what's *that* mean?" Audrey demanded of the world in general, when Joan had silently walked out, just as she always did walk: slowly, with head a little down, eyebrows a little raised, toes a little pointed. There were some people, oddly enough, who found that slightly strutting, extremely self-satisfied walk the most irritating thing in the world.

"She must have done something," Philippa suggested: but half-heartedly, because Joan very rarely "did" anything.

"The grandfather's gone bankrupt!" Alison cried excitedly. "Or somebody's dead!"

"Not he!" said Audrey. "Joan isn't the sort of person that unpleasant things *really* happen to. If she was, she'd give up finding a fresh grievance round every corner."

Katharine, always the kindest of the kind, made a suggestion which simultaneously offered a reason and threw the cloak of charity over Joan's behaviour.

"I didn't think, when she came in, that she was looking a bit well," she said anxiously. "Do you think, perhaps, she's— she's sickening? and might that be why she wasn't very—very jolly?"

"Who ever knew Joan Grouse *jolly!*" Audrey exclaimed derisively. But there was just enough possibility in the idea to make everyone look a little serious. Measles was so rife in the school, that Miss Crewe had definitely forbidden the word to be mentioned, since she had found it discussed and dwelt upon most unwholesomely in every direction. And there hadn't been a case for ten days; and half-term was so very near. ...

Stella, always a gloomy soul, made a fresh suggestion that was even more depressing.

"Suppose it went dragging on till the end of the term," she said, "and we were still in quarantine—would you be able to go to Constantinople, Peggy?"

"Oh, *help!*" Audrey cried: for Peggy was an impressionable person, easily given to tears, and her eyes were already filling at the awful thought. "Stella, go and put your head in a bag! Why, it's seven weeks off!"

"But why *does* the Captain want Joan?" Stella persisted, in her irritating fashion.

"Goodness knows!" said Audrey. "At any rate, *we* don't: so let's go on about what we were saying before."

They went on about what they were saying before; and it speedily became so absorbing, that time flew unheeded. When the dinner-bell rang, everyone was astonished; and the same question came spontaneously from more than one mouth.

"It *can't* be as late as that! What on earth has Joan been away all this time for?"

CHAPTER II

Why Joan Was Wanted

MISS CREWE (who was naturally called The Captain) was not in the drawing-room when Joan arrived there; but this was not at all surprising. It was, in fact, her habit to let the summoned person find an empty room, and have a brief interval to meditate on her guilty past. In the present instance, Joan had no sense of guilt, and therefore very little uneasiness: though such a summons is, of course, always slightly alarming, and there may always be some old forgotten sin that has been suddenly brought to light. But, as has already been said, she was not an habitual sinner; so she felt free to look about her, and see what was to be seen. It was an attractive room, with comfortable furniture that was also good to look at, pictures that one liked to see more than once, flowers that seemed always freshly gathered, and plenty of books that were obviously well read. Joan turned to a couple of new ones that lay on a table near; for she liked reading, and it was refreshing to see something that wasn't School Library.

The top one was extremely dull: a book of essays that might have been sermons, or of sermons that might have been essays. Wishing that Miss Crewe were not quite so awfully clever (as she undoubtedly was), Joan looked at the underneath book; and that wasn't fiction either. It had pictures, however: the queerest pictures. It was called "Our Mothers"; and it appeared to describe, with a wealth of illustration, the extraordinary life that people apparently led at the end of the eighteen-hundreds. Of course everyone knows, in a vague way, that that benighted age had no motors or wireless or cinemas, or—or anything, in fact; but these pictures, and the descriptions of them, did bring it home in the most amazing way. ... Joan sat down, with the book in her lap, and forgot time.

"I'm so sorry to have kept you waiting like this, Joan," said Miss Crewe, coming in at last with what appeared, to the absorbed Joan, great suddenness. "I was unexpectedly hindered."

As a matter of fact, a suspected person had suddenly confessed to spots, and was now weeping upstairs in the sick-rooms with a bad headache; but Miss Crewe had no idea of mentioning this. For one thing, she was not the sort of ruler who makes laws and then breaks them herself: for another, the last girl in the school to whom she would willingly have divulged the unpleasant news was this self-centred, spoilt Joan Partridge.

"It's—it's quite all right," said Joan. (How *does* one suitably answer one's head-mistress, when she makes a sort of apology?)

"I'm glad you found such an interesting book," said Miss Crewe. "Rather hard to realise what things were like in those days, isn't it? ... Oh, of course I was born in those times myself; but I don't pretend to remember them!"

She laughed: being one of those rare and sensible people who didn't mind anyone knowing that she was forty-five.

"It is ... awfully interesting and—and queer," said Joan.

"I'm sending it to an aunt of mine, who was about your age in those days," said Miss Crewe. "Now, if you were to meet her, *she* could tell you all sorts of things ..."

She stopped abruptly.

"Perhaps you may meet her," she said, in a rather odd voice.

"I should love to," said Joan politely. She was wondering very much what could be the reason for all this unnecessary book-chat; for usually Miss Crewe went straight to her point, and wasted no words when she got there. ... Of course it might be interesting to meet the unknown aunt. Was she coming to stay? In that case, would Joan be invited to Sunday tea in the drawing-room? She hadn't been, all this term. Katharine had been, *twice* …

"Joan," said Miss Crewe, suddenly and abruptly. "I'm sorry to say that I've just had a telegram from your mother … no, she isn't ill! None of your people are ill. But you can't go home for half-term."

"Not go *home!*" Joan gasped. (But she *always* went home. Mummy wasn't one of those heartless mothers who occasionally went away themselves, and fobbed off their unfortunate daughters upon some relation. And, if no one was ill, *why* …?)

"One of your maids has developed scarlet fever; and, of course, you must keep away while the house is in quarantine," said Miss Crewe.

"It … it *is* hard luck!" said Joan, on the verge of tears. (Mummy always did such a *lot* for her at half-term: Lord's, and a matinée, and all sorts of things.)

Miss Crewe glanced at her oddly.

"Yes, very hard luck … as you say. Most upsetting and trying for your mother; and the poor girl herself is probably feeling not only ill, but horribly guilty for giving so much trouble: though I daresay it wasn't her fault at all."

This hadn't, of course, been Joan's point of view in the least. The hard luck was, in her opinion, entirely her own: disappointing her of three days at home, and all sorts of fun, at three days' notice.

"Here is the telegram," said Miss Crewe, a little abruptly.

She was not, Joan felt, sympathetic *at all*; but, of course, that was the way in which people always did behave. … She took the flimsy pink sheet, and read.

"Kitchen-maid developed scarlet fever to-day. Can you arrange Joan's half-term? So sorry to give trouble."

"Mummy always *said* she looked delicate," was Joan's only comment, in a most injured voice.

"Is she a new maid?"

Miss Crewe's tone was very dry.

"Oh, no! She's a younger sister of my old nurse, who is Mummy's maid now."

"You know her quite well, then?"

"Oh, yes! She came from my grandfather's, in Shropshire; her father's a gamekeeper."

"Well, it is to be hoped that the infection will not spread in the house," said Miss Crewe, more drily than ever.

Joan opened eyes of horror, and said: "Oh, *yes!*" in a heartfelt tone. That, of course, would be really terrible; and it hadn't occurred to her as a possibility until this moment—she never saw much farther than her very immediate surroundings. Why, it might go on from one to another, till it even interfered with the summer holidays! She turned quite cold at the thought. This half-term business was bad enough; but not to be compared with the awfulness of summer holidays without Mummy, or ... or all the usual people and things that combined to make for pleasure.

"Well," said Miss Crewe, in a brisk, business-like way, after an inexplicable little pause—she might, Joan thought vaguely, have been almost waiting for some special comment to be made—"Well, as it happens, this aunt of mine—whom I mentioned to you before—is kind enough occasionally to take in one or two girls who are unprovided for, like you. Of course, this is very short notice, and she may not be able to have you. I will ring her up at once and inquire; and let you know."

Joan's face, long enough before, dropped a little more. Wasn't it rather an awful prospect? If the aunt was pretty old, she might be—probably was—stiff and dull. She might live in some quite horrid place ...

"She lives at Slonsea," said Miss Crewe at that very moment, exactly as if she had been reading Joan's private thoughts: an uncanny habit that she had.

"Oh!" said Joan, a little feebly.

"You don't know it? Oh, a nice south-coast seaside place; I used to love staying there, when I was your age," said Miss Crewe. "Good bathing: splendid public baths: good shops— all that sort of thing, and lovely country round. *If* she can have you, I've no doubt about your enjoying yourself; everyone likes my Aunt Maggie. I wish I had a photograph of her to show you; but she hates being taken—so I've only *this!*"

She laughed, as she took a large old-fashioned album from a high shelf; turned over the thick leaves rapidly, and then put it down before Maggie: a very old-fashioned picture of a bright-faced girl, with dark hair tied back with a ribbon, and a hideous high-necked dress. fastened with a brooch, standing behind an elderly lady wearing a cap and looking down at a book.

"I'm not so sure whether you would have cared to stay with my Great-Aunt Margaret, who *was* strict, in the old-fashioned manner—though very kind," said Miss Crewe, looking at the face under the cap. "But Aunt Maggie, though of course you'd think her pretty old, is a delightful person." She went on to give details about the house, and where it was, and things of that sort. ... "Well, I think that's all, Joan," she ended. "I'll ring her up at once. And then I'll ring your mother up—the reason she telegraphed, of course, was because she knows that I never answer the telephone in school-hours—and let her know. And then I'll tell you what has been arranged."

"Thank you, Miss Crewe," said Joan.

She didn't look at all thankful. She looked like a thoroughly cross, injured, self-centred person of fifteen, with a grievance that she felt to be more than justified, and tears very near the surface.

"You may go up to your room, if you like; and I'll send a message there," said Miss Crewe. She was always, perhaps, unusually lenient with this exasperating pupil, just because she found her so exasperating and wished to be strictly just.

"Thank you, Miss Crewe," said Joan again.

She stalked slowly away—head down, eyebrows a little raised, toes a little pointed—and Miss Crewe, when the door was safely shut, gave a laugh that was very nearly a groan. She had had difficult girls before: plenty of them. But she had never had one so complacently shut up in a hard armour of self-love and self-pity.

"*Poor* Aunt Maggie!" she said, looking down affectionately at the open album. And then she put it away on its high shelf, and turned to her telephone.

Twenty minutes later, Joan received her message. She had spent the intervening time lying on her bed, screwing out difficult tears by thinking, hard, what an injured person she was: never once thinking of the anxious, trying time that her mother was enduring, or of the miserable sick girl in the Isolation Hospital. It was a shame! Only, of course, what she might have expected: she, who always had hard luck, and whom everyone conspired to … "Come in!"

"Miss Crewe asked me to say, Miss, that she has rung up on the 'phone, and it's all quite satisfactory."

"Thank you," Joan muttered glumly; and put her head down on the pillow again, and pumped up some more tears. All quite satisfactory, indeed! Miss Crewe might think so, and the unknown seaside aunt might think so, and even Mummy might think so—they *would*. But Joan herself, that pitiful martyr who never got any sympathy, was jolly well going to lie here and cry hard, so that she might be quite unfit to go back to the society of other girls. She might as well, in fact, get into bed at once. She had quite a promising headache already, and her throat felt lumpy and thick. By the time anyone came up to see what she was about, she proposed to be found undressed and limp, obviously too unwell to do anything but stay peacefully in bed until the morning.

CHAPTER III

LEGS

THE train seemed very slow; and it was hot; and no one, surely (except Joan Partridge), had ever travelled with such impossible fellow-passengers. They were all so odd; and yet not with any sort of oddness that made them, in Joan's eyes, interesting.

Opposite her sat an old lady in most old-fashioned clothes. Indeed, perhaps it was her clothes that made her look older than she was, for her face was quite smooth and unwrinkled, and she had a nice pink colour in her cheeks. But she wore a bonnet, such as only very old ladies wear, with black strings that tied under her chin; and a curious mantle that seemed to keep her arms pinned to her sides; and black stockings, and black boots—*boots*, on a hot summer day! Her skirt was black too, and long, touching the dusty floor. She looked at Joan once or twice—or not exactly at Joan, but at Joan's legs. They didn't seem to please the old lady at all; and yet a hasty inspection made their owner sure that there was no visible hole in her stockings, and that they weren't wrinkled or twisted, or in any way unseemly. To be sure, her summer coat *was* rather short; she had meant to point this out at once, as soon as she got home, and then Mummy would take her to buy another. . . .

She wasn't going home. It was the first day of the half-term holiday; and she was sitting in a hot South-coast train, on her way to the unknown aunt of Miss Crewe, who might prove perfectly *foul*. And she would have to go on wearing that too-short coat all the rest of the term. What bad luck she always had!

She turned a lack-lustre eye to the other end of the carriage, so that she might avoid that glare from across the way. Beastly rude, really, of the old lady, to stare like that! At her age, she ought to have known better.

Two men faced each other by the window on the far side. One, Joan thought, must be a Dissenting minister: not that she knew any, but this was her general idea of what they might be expected to look like. He was all in very severe black, with a long full coat—very hot, one would have thought, on such a day. His hat was a queer, squashy, clerical-looking thing of black felt, like nothing Joan had ever seen before: low and flat, with a wide brim. He had a straggly beard, so thin that his collar could be seen through it: not the ordinary round collar that one expects of a parson, but an odd low one, fastening in front, with a white tie. He was writing something, which seemed to require thought, in a note-book: looking up at intervals to meditate, and then down again to jot down a few words—undoubtedly a sermon, and a long one, too. Joan hoped that he was not going to Slonsea, or that at any rate she was not going to listen to him on Sunday. He did not take any notice of her at all; but then he was on her side of the carriage.

The man opposite to him was quite different, but also odd. His hair wanted cutting; and he wore a check cap, rather on the back of his head. His knickerbocker suit was of the same loud and rather vulgar check; and, though it was undoubtedly a knickerbocker suit, in some way it was quite different from any plus-fours that Joan had ever seen—tighter-fitting, and, oh! *quite* different. He had a round face, a cheeky smile, and a thick moustache; and the cheeky smile was directed, more often than was at all pleasant, to Joan's legs. It really made her feel quite hot and uncomfortable. She gave the short coat a surreptitious pull, to make it come lower: but without success. She glared stiffly at the man; and he instantly put up a picture-paper, of a very vulgar nature—some paper that Joan had never previously seen or heard of, depicting an old man with a white hat and a large bulbous nose—between her and him, grinning at her occasionally from behind it in a perfectly hateful manner.

She looked haughtily away: and had the good luck—for once—to have her attention at once distracted by something she had never seen before: a large 2 on the door of the carriage. What a very strange railway this seemed to be! Such unusual fellow-passengers, and second-class carriages that, of course, were never found anywhere. Having an inquiring mind, Joan had once asked of somebody why there was nothing but First and Third, and been told that Second used also to exist, once upon a time, but had fallen so much into disuse that they had been abolished.

At that point the train stopped at a Junction, and tickets were inspected (by a ticket-collector with a beard), and Joan's enemy at the far end was discovered to be travelling with a third-class ticket, and was ignominiously expelled. That was, at least, something. She breathed more freely when he and his comic paper had departed, in such a whirl of indignation that he had not time for even a parting glance at her legs.

His place was taken by another young man with a moustache—what an extraordinarily hairy country the South Coast seemed to be! Joan thought—who almost instantly found that he knew the old lady opposite, and came to sit by her. He wore white, flannels and a blazer, and carried a tennis-racquet of a rather odd shape; but, except for that, there was nothing unusual about him (by this time Joan was beginning to expect the unusual, quite as a matter of course) except the way he talked: a South-coast accent, she supposed. The letter R appeared to be unknown to him, and he cut out all his final G's. He had been, it appeared, in America—perhaps he had picked it up there?—and he hadn't seen the old lady since last

December. On which her very odd comment was, that she *still* found it difficult to get used to ninety—but, of course, one had got so used to the eighties

As far as politeness permitted, Joan stared at her. She *couldn't* be as old as that! In spite of her bonnet and her old-fashioned clothes, her face was still so very smooth and pink. The young man, however, without any appearance of surprise, quite agreed with her: though Joan couldn't help feeling that it would have been more tactful to express a justifiable surprise at her age. He went on to say, in answer to a question, that he had hardly been playin' tennis at all this season; he'd been stayin' with an uncle in Dorset, and widin' a good deal. Joan was so enthralled by his accent, that she only realised with a start, when the train was absolutely standing still, that the station they had reached was Slonsea.

None of her fellow-passengers was getting out, but the black-coated clerical gentleman was very polite about opening the door for her. The last words she heard, however, were from the young man at the far end, saying, in a rather lowered voice, that something was "weally wathah wum," and the old lady's answer that *she* called it hardly decent. Joan had a horrid feeling that both these remarks referred to her legs; and she got away from the neighbourhood of the carriage as fast as possible.

"Luggage, Miss?" said a porter with a queer fringe of beard under his chin; and Joan told him Yes, a suit-case with J.R.P. on it. (She couldn't imagine why Mademoiselle, setting her off, hadn't had it put in the carriage with her, which would have saved trouble now; but Mademoiselle always was rather flustered by stations and tickets.)

"A *what*, Miss?"

"One suit-case," Joan repeated clearly; but he still didn't seem to understand—an exceptionally stupid man. He suggested her picking it out for herself from the luggage that had been tumbled out on the platform—very singular luggage indeed. There were great black ark-like things with domed lids, some of amazing size. There were solid leather trunks that looked as if they weighed tons. There were extraordinary long, narrow things, made apparently out of old pieces of carpet, with leather handles. But of Joan's neat green case with the Zip fastening—or, indeed, of anything remotely like it—there was no sign.

"It—it isn't here," she said blankly. (How *awful* to arrive in a strange house with no luggage!)

The porter, who was very well-meaning in spite of his stupidity, went and rummaged in the van; but there was nothing left behind there. The train moved off. Joan looked round to see if anyone was there to meet her; and there was no one who seemed in the least likely. Indeed, the few people there had already, during this delay, met the friends they expected, and collected their luggage, and were going away; and nobody was looking out for a stray schoolgirl. Joan felt injured and aggrieved.

"Please call a taxi!" she said loftily to the porter.

He didn't seem to understand. He stared, and asked her to say it again; and then went away rather suddenly and talked to another porter, both of them staring back at her. Joan had a sudden horrid feeling that they were discussing her short coat and long legs. She walked very hastily to the exit, gave up her ticket to a collector with (of course) a moustache, and found herself outside the station.

There were no taxis there—of course the earlier people had taken them all. The only vehicles left were three very unattractive old-fashioned cabs with extremely ancient horses; so it was a mercy that Miss Crewe had happened to mention the comforting fact that her aunt lived very near the station. Joan inquired the way of a rosy old woman in a sunbonnet, and set off without any undue haste: head a little down, eyebrows a little raised, toes a little pointed. She was, of course, meeting with worse luck than would have fallen to anyone else's share: a horrid journey, lost luggage, no one to meet her. She wasn't at all prepared to like Slonsea, or Miss Crewe's aunt, or anything at all connected with her half-term holiday.

CHAPTER IV

CALISTHENIC DRESS

WELLINGTON SQUARE, Slonsea, is not a Square at all, being much longer than it is broad: which, as all maths-mistresses will tell you, is absurd. It begins near the station, runs down a rather steep hill, and then proceeds at a very gentle slope towards the sea-front, broadening a good deal just before it gets there. It has good tall imposing houses on both sides, and perfectly dull gardens, with tennis-courts, in the middle; and only people living in the Square are allowed to enter the gardens, or, consequently, play tennis there.

Number Sixty-one was on the darker side, facing east, near the sea; and there Joan, after due inquiries, made her way. She thought, during that brief walk, that Slonsea was the dullest place she had ever seen in her life: quite incredibly dull, with quite incredibly uninteresting-looking people about. There was almost no traffic. She had not seen a decent car since she left the station; she didn't believe, in fact, that she had seen a car of any sort. The old-fashioned, dowdy people whom she met stared at her in a bewildered sort of way, as if she were a freak. It seemed to Joan, who had become sensitive on the subject, that they all looked pointedly at her legs. She was quite sensibly relieved to get off the pavement, and mount a steepish flight of steps, and ring an old-fashioned pulley-bell, which clanged and jingled audibly inside the house as she rang it. Probably, she thought disdainfully, they hadn't discovered electricity down here, yet! And she looked at the lamp that happened to be just opposite, and found to her amazement that she was quite right. It was a gas-lamp.

The door was opened, as might have been expected, by

an old-fashioned-looking servant, wearing a long black dress, a large plain bib-apron, and a very large cap. ... And yet she looked quite young! She told Joan that Mrs. Corrie was at home, and asked her to step this way, please. And Joan, stepping that way, was ushered into a large, rather dark, sitting-room facing east over the Square.

"Miss Partridge, ma'am."

"Why, my dear!" said Mrs. Corrie, "didn't Maggie meet you at the station?"

No question could have been easier to answer; and yet Joan found herself practically destitute of speech. It was such a— such an incredible room: such queer old-fashioned furniture, such a queer fire-place, such queer gas-globes in the middle, set in a chandelier. And Mrs. Corrie herself—well, the first thing that came to Joan's mind was, that she was like pictures of Queen Victoria. There wasn't, really, very much personal likeness, and Mrs. Corrie was undoubtedly not nearly so old; it was principally the cap—Joan had never seen anyone wearing one before. A large, high lace cap, mounted on black velvet, with a little mauve ribbon for trimming. ... As a matter of fact, there was a picture of Queen Victoria on the wall, so comparison was quite easy.

"Didn't Maggie ...?" Mrs. Corrie was beginning again, in a tone of mild surprise; for it really was rather strange to see a girl standing at the door, goggling at her like that. But she was interrupted, and the question was rendered superfluous, by the sound of the violent opening and shutting of the front door, agitated footsteps in the hall, and a breathless voice.

"Mother, I *am* sorry! Fräulein simply *would* keep me. And I ran every step of the way to the station and she wasn't ... *Oh!*"

The voice broke off suddenly in an astounded gasp. Joan turned to see the speaker. They stood staring at each other.

The newcomer, as we know, saw a thinnish girl in a coat that was too short for her: a girl with neatly bobbed hair, and the usual little hat pulled tightly down over it: a girl with rather long legs in the usual beige stockings, and a pair of very good lizard shoes that were the pride of their owner's heart.

Joan saw, for her part, a girl of about her own age and height, but very much—well, fatter, certainly; but, apart from that, of a perfectly different shape: rounded out, and drawn in, and entirely different from the straight up-and-down effect that is now usual. She had long hair, drawn back from her face, and tied behind with a ribbon; and it was quite easy to see all this, because her hat—a sailor hat, like what is technically described as a Gent's Straw Boater—was perched in the most extraordinary manner on the very top of her head. Joan could not imagine how it ever stayed there, for apparently the lightest puff of wind would send it flying. She wore a cotton frock, so high at the neck that it ended somewhere near her ears, with a lacy sort of frill, and so long that it reached her ankles; and there Joan's eyes, having once reached that spot, remained riveted—it met high, black, buttoned *boots*. Boots—*black* boots—black boots on a very hot summer afternoon!

"This is my daughter Maggie," Mrs. Corrie was saying, when Joan had sufficiently recovered from all these shocks to hear anything. "She is just your age, Joan; and I hope you will have a happy time together for this short holiday."

Joan murmured, in a dazed voice: "Thank you." The other girl was simultaneously murmuring something to the same effect, in the same sort of tone.

"And now, my dear, what about your luggage?"

"I am most terribly sorry," Joan apologised. "But it—it somehow didn't come with me. I can't *think* why ..."

It was, of course, inevitable that Mrs. Corrie should look at her legs as she answered, in a rather constrained voice, that that was a pity. It might, perhaps, arrive by an early train to-morrow, if it had been accidentally left behind at the last moment. She (rather emphatically) *hoped* so. Maggie could, of course, lend a night-dress and a brush and comb; and Joan would like, of course, to go up to her room now and wash before tea.

Maggie took her up; and Joan, following, had her fascinated eyes on the black button-boots. This was her room; and Maggie's was next door, if she wanted anything; and Maggie *was* sorry about the luggage—horrid for her!

Joan walked in, looking about her.

It was quite a nice room, looking out in front with a sideways view of the sea; but in some way it was—different—from any room that she had ever slept in before. The bed had a high back, and back-and-side curtains of a queer dull-red stuff that felt rough when she touched it, and a valance all round of the same; and there were curtains at the window to match. There were also blinds made of horizontal slats of wood, that let the light through in streaks. There was not much furniture: just the things that were necessary: no book-shelf, or writing-table, or easy-chair of any sort. It was, in fact, a room made strictly for sleeping and dressing in, not intended for the spending of any leisure time. The furniture was rather large and heavy and dull: all except the dressing-table, which was surprisingly frivolous. It was high and flat, and covered with white muslin, which hung down to the ground all round like a petticoat. Under the muslin—Joan had the curiosity to look and see—was an under-petticoat of something that she had never met before: stiff, thick, cotton stuff with a highly glazed surface, of the very brightest pink.

Maggie knocked and came in.

"I've brought you a brush and comb, and a night-dress. ..."

She broke off suddenly, staring; and then appeared to feel that she was rude, and coloured almost as brightly as the pink table-cover, and asked in an odd voice if Joan was ready for tea, and took her downstairs again.

Tea was laid in the dining-room: a rather dark room at the back, with large, heavy mahogany furniture, and an extremely queer wallpaper: dark-red and woolly-looking, feeling quite soft and thick to the hand, as Joan accidentally touched it in passing. It was a very nice tea, with jam, and shrimps, and three sorts of cake; but that was not why Joan sat down hurriedly. It was Mrs. Corrie's look of utter surprise and dismay, pausing for a moment with the uplifted tea-pot in her hand, when she saw the two girls at the door. She drew in her lips rather alarmingly for a minute, and her voice sounded constrained as she asked Joan about sugar; but after that, all appeared to be well, and tea took its normal course. Joan was hungry, and made a very good meal.

They returned to the drawing-room, Joan following modestly in Mrs. Corrie's wake; and as she followed, she wondered. She had got more or less used to the cap by this time; but she hadn't realised the extraordinary dress. It wasn't so much that it was very long, reaching the ground—dresses were, she knew quite well, getting surprisingly long nowadays; but its shape was so exceedingly queer. Like Maggie's, it was very high at the throat, ending in a lace frill; the top part of it was quite tight-fitting, sloping in to a real waist; the skirt was enormous, pleated and frilled, and sticking out in the most unnatural manner at the back. It must, Joan considered with astonishment, have taken simply yards and yards of stuff; and the effect was, in her eyes, hideous.

It was a lovely evening, the sun shining on the Square and on the sea beyond in the most tantalising manner; but there seemed no idea of going out. Mrs. Corrie sat down in her chair by the window, and took up some very plain sewing, and began to talk to Joan.

Maggie, after some murmured instructions from her mother outside the door, had slipped away.

"I didn't know, my dear, that you had been ill."

"I haven't," said Joan, rather taken aback.

"*Not* been ill?"

Mrs. Corrie surveyed her with surprise: her hair, her drill-slip, and (of course) her legs. ... Joan couldn't imagine, by the way, what had induced her to travel in her drill-slip. All very well to *bring* it, of course, for it might come in handy on the beach—but not to wear it for arrival. There must have been a terrible rush at the last moment—though she couldn't remember it—and she hadn't had time to change. But perhaps Mrs. Corrie thought it bad manners not to have come properly dressed for the afternoon. ... However, it was still worse manners not to answer; so she hastened to do so.

"No. There's been measles at the school, of course, almost ever since the beginning of term; but *I* haven't had it—or anything else!"

"*Really?*" said Mrs. Corrie. "But your hair, my dear! And your calisthenic dress is so *very* short!"

Joan felt affronted. As a matter of fact, her drill-slip, new this term, had been a trifle over the regulation length, to her extreme annoyance. ... And *what* had Mrs. Corrie called it?

"Do you mean this?" she said, touching it. "Oh, no, Mrs. Corrie, it isn't, really! We all have just the same length; it's the school uniform."

"The school *what?*" said Mrs. Corrie.

"The school *uniform,*" Joan repeated, a little louder. (Perhaps her hostess was really old enough to be a little deaf.)

Mrs. Corrie looked so odd—bewildered, and unbelieving, and even annoyed—that it was quite uncomfortable to go on facing her. Joan, looking out of the window for relief, saw to her surprise Maggie, running up the house steps very fast, with a little white parcel in her hand. She came in, still a little breathless with haste.

"I've brought you a tooth-brush," she said, offering it.

"Oh—thanks very much!" said Joan, once more taken

aback. "But why didn't you ask me to come too? I'd have loved to go out!"

Maggie, turning red, looked at her mother; and there was an awkward little pause.

"My dear," said Mrs. Corrie, gently but decidedly, "you could not possibly have gone out like that."

"Like *this?*" said Joan, staring. "But we always go out like this!"

"Out of the *house?* In your calisthenic dress?" said Mrs. Corrie. And, if she had been accusing Joan of going out without any dress at all, she couldn't have looked more shocked.

"Why, of course!" said Joan. She turned to Maggie. "Don't *you?*"

Maggie, for her part, was actually blushing.

"No, indeed!" she said, with vigour. "And mine is *much* longer than yours—I'll show you!"

In the couple of minutes that she was gone, there was a very constrained silence; and it continued, on Joan's part, after the return of Maggie and the dress. Such a garment! It was in two distinct parts: blue serge knickers, a loose blue dress to match, with long sleeves and a rather high neck. As Maggie held it up against herself, it came half-way down her legs.

"I shouldn't *think* of going out in it!" she said, quite indignantly.

"No," said Joan, in a non-committal voice. "I shouldn't think you would." (Why, she herself wouldn't have been seen dead anywhere in such an appalling garment!)

"We change at school, of course, for calisthenics," said Maggie; "and then change back again. I've only got it at home because a bit of the hem came undone."

"You change for *what?*" said Joan.

"Calisthenics, of course!"

"What *is* that?" Joan inquired further.

"Don't you have them at your school?" said Maggie, looking

shocked and superior. "Well, they *are* rather new! Indian clubs—and dumb-bells—and wands—and chest-expanders."

"What are they?" Joan demanded, devoured by curiosity.

"I've got mine at home. Look!"

Joan looked, with very round eyes, at two round rings of a reddish varnished wood, joined by a length of doubled red ribbon with, apparently, elastic inside.

"What on earth do you do with those?" she inquired faintly.

"Well, see!"

Maggie showed her, quite proudly: taking a ring in each hand and doing arm-exercises with them. It really didn't look bad fun. The elastic pulled her arms pretty tautly together, and didn't allow of any stooping when it was behind her back. Nor indeed did the long slender stick which she presently produced as her "wand." ... But what Kindergarten baby games for a girl of her age!

"And is that all you do?" Joan asked.

"Of course not! We run, and march, and jump ..."

"It's just a sort of drill, then?" said Joan, grasping this at last.

"It's *calisthenics*," said Maggie.

"And do you have parallel bars, and a vaulting horse, and ropes?" Joan asked, thinking of the well-fitted gymnasium at St. Aldate's.

"I never heard of them!" Maggie answered, rather blankly. "What are they for?"

"Well—gym.!" said Joan.

Mrs. Corrie turned reproving eyes upon her, over the tops of her reading-glasses.

"And what," she asked repressively, "is a *gym.?*"

CHAPTER V

A DIFFICULT DATE

BY the time that Joan had finished explaining, very inefficiently, the meaning of "gym," to two people who had never heard of such a thing and (obviously) didn't quite believe her, she was most thoroughly subdued. Maggie's incredible school, it appeared, didn't wear uniform of any sort. She went to school in the sort of frock she was wearing now; and the other girls also wore what they—or their parents—chose. There were no Houses, no badges, not even a hat-ribbon—not even, in fact, a school hat! Most of the girls wore the straw sailors that she was wearing; but there was no particular reason why they should not, if the fancy took them, appear in a large fussy feathered hat, such as Joan had noticed passing the window more than once. Having finished her explanation, she sat looking out, very quiet. If Mrs. Corrie so entirely disapproved of her drill-slip, and her suit-case didn't turn up, she seemed likely to spend the whole of her holiday indoors: an appalling prospect. And it was such a lovely evening! She watched, with a lump in her throat, the housemaid running up the area steps in front, with a quick glance back at the house, and running to the pillar-box at the Square corner, and running back again very fast indeed. Lucky girl! *Her* skirt was right down to her ankles, and even Mrs. Corrie couldn't …

"Ring the bell, please, Maggie," said Mrs. Corrie at that moment; and put aside her plain sewing, and got up from her seat opposite Joan, and went quietly out into the hall. They could hear her speaking to the housemaid. They could hear an answer that sounded agitated: that quite obviously, after a moment, broke into tears.

"She *will* do it," said Maggie, rather uncomfortably.

"Who does what?" Joan inquired, quite at sea.

"Sarah. She *will* run out to the post without asking leave."

"But why shouldn't she?" asked Joan blankly.

"Well, of *course* not!" said Maggie, shocked. "She has her afternoon off, once a week, and she goes to church once every Sunday. She isn't supposed to go out at any other time. Mother said, when she did it last, that she couldn't keep her if she went on behaving like that."

"But—does your mother ever keep *any* servants?" Joan asked, more blankly still.

"Of course she does!" said Maggie, affronted. "This is a very good place; our maids generally stay for ages, till they marry. Mother is strict, of course; but she's very good to them. Now Miss Home, next door, does find it difficult to get maids; but then she is very old-fashioned, and she *will* make them wear bonnets when they go out."

"*Bonnets?*" Joan repeated, dazed: with a mental vision of the very fine young ladies in silk stockings and all the latest fashions, whom she had seen issuing from her home in London on Sundays and most other days.

Maggie nodded.

"The old-fashioned plain bonnets with a plain ribbon. Of course all servants used to wear them; but they won't now. Miss Home says she can't think what they are coming to."

It occurred to Joan that she herself could have given Miss Home all sorts of information on that subject; but she didn't suggest doing so. If Mrs. Corrie were reckoned an ordinary "good mistress," Miss Home must be a Tartar indeed.

Mrs. Corrie, coming quietly back, suggested that Maggie should give them a little music; and Maggie, looking rather shy, opened the piano obediently, and played something called "Sea Memories," and then a Chopin waltz. She did not seem to enjoy it at all; and she played rather badly, with a good many wrong notes.

"Thank you, dear," said Mrs. Corrie. "Now, Joan, what are you going to give us? Can you play without your music? If not, I daresay Maggie has something that you know."

"I'm afraid I can't play at all," said Joan.

Mrs. Corrie smiled; but there was a little severity in her face.

"That is being *too* modest," she said. "We shall not be at all critical—Maggie, as you have heard, is not a great performer herself."

"I *do* practise," Maggie murmured lamentably.

"I know you do, my dear; you are very good about it, and you know Fräulein thinks you are improving. ... Now, Joan."

"But I can't play *at all*," Joan repeated wildly. "I'm not a bit musical—I've never learnt!"

"Do you mean that you've been allowed to give it up?" Maggie inquired, enviously and incredulously.

"I never *began* to learn," said Joan, with an uncomfortable look at Mrs. Corrie: whose expression was a little stern and more than a little shocked.

"But see, my dear," she said, "how much pleasure you miss yourself, and how much you fail to give other people!"

It occurred to Joan (but she was far too much crushed even to hint as much) that Maggie had not appeared to enjoy herself extravagantly at the piano, and that any really musical person would have found her performance very trying. Joan did, however, put up a mild fight.

"My mother is *very* musical," she said. "She couldn't bear to listen to any music that wasn't really good."

Mrs. Corrie's eyebrows rose a little.

"I am surprised, in that case," she said, "that you don't try to learn and give her pleasure."

"It *wouldn't* give her pleasure," said Joan bluntly. "She said herself that it was no good for me to learn! And why should

I? We have an awfully good gramophone, and a four-valve wireless!"

If she had said that they had an awfully good elephant and a four-legged chicken, her hostesses couldn't have looked at her with more complete amazement. She might have been talking some foreign language of which they knew nothing.

"I'm afraid we don't quite understand you, Joan," said Mrs. Corrie. "In any case, it is time now for Maggie to do her lying-down; and I always read to her while she does it."

"Oh, Mother! Must I, to-night?" Maggie asked, again a little lamentably.

"Yes, my dear, of course. I will go and fetch the book," said Mrs. Corrie; and went out of the room, while Maggie obediently, but rather dismally, took a cushion from the sofa, and arranged herself flat on the floor.

"Why do you have to do that?" Joan inquired.

"Mother thought I was stooping rather; and of course this *is* the best way to stop it, I suppose," Maggie answered from the floor.

"Why don't you have massage?"

"What's that?" Maggie asked hopefully, raising her, head from the cushion. "Some sort of medicine?"

"No, no! Rubbing—by a proper masseuse."

"But I don't know what *that* is," said Maggie blankly; and then in a hurry, as Mrs. Corrie's step was heard on the stairs, "I say! Do you mean that you never learnt *any* music, or had to practise *at all?*"

"Of course I never did. I told you so."

"You *lucky!*" Maggie exclaimed, with a great envious gust of a sigh.

"Do you have to do much of it?" Joan inquired hurriedly. (Mrs. Corrie had stopped to speak to someone in the hall; but she might come in at any moment.)

"Two and a half hours a day, now. It used to be only two; but Fräulein said I was getting on so slowly ..."

Maggie's raised head fell back, as her mother came in with a book in her hand.

"We are reading L. T. Meade's ' Polly,'" she said to Joan. "I hope you have not read it? It only came out last year."

"No," Joan said, in a bewildered voice. "I ... I haven't read it."

(L. T. Meade? Wasn't she as old as the hills? One met a book or two of hers, handed down from people's mothers. How *could* she have published a book last year?)

"It's such a jolly book!" said Maggie, settling herself comfortably to listen. And Joan, for her part, was quite content to be quiet and listen too—and try, if possible, to get her muddled thoughts into some sort of order. Everything seemed so—so *queer*. She might almost have travelled to another world: a strange, stiff world, where she didn't understand and wasn't understood. It was all most perplexing. ...

How very well Mrs. Corrie read! And the book was, in a queer way, very interesting—a queer old-fashioned way, Joan would have said without hesitation, if she hadn't been definitely told that it was a last year's book. People didn't behave like that nowadays! Servants didn't talk like that; old family cooks *certainly* were not to be had for twenty-two pounds a year—Joan remembered plaintive wails of her mother's on that subject. Doctors weren't driven in "carriages"; they drove themselves in their own cars. What was the "rickety fly" in which Aunt Maria arrived? And what, if you came to that, was a toy-terrier?

"Thank you, Mother," said Maggie at last, when the reading came to an end; and Joan was able truthfully to say that she had enjoyed it. The time had really gone so fast that she was surprised to hear the bell ringing for supper; but of course seven o'clock *was* early—too early for her to be very hungry, not having been out. Things were very nice, however: though it was a surprise, when they went back to the drawing-room, to find that the windows had been closely shut. Not only that. All along the top of the lower sashes—they were heavy bay-windows—lay strange fat scarlet sausages, like immense breakfast-sausages covered in red cloth. Maggie saw Joan's glance at them.

"Don't you have those at your home? I don't expect you get such winds as we do here! The draughts used to come in most dreadfully, until Mother got those things—you ought to tell your mother about them."

Joan said nothing; there was nothing, in fact, that she could say politely, her own mother being rather delicate and a fresh-air fanatic. The room seemed to her terribly stuffy—and the light outside was still so bright and alluring! But Mrs. Corrie, far from suggesting a last run by the sea, very soon suggested bed instead—yes, bed at eight o'clock on a fine summer evening. Joan stared at her, thinking it must be a joke; but it was not, and Maggie evidently took it quite as a matter of course.

"Now, not too much talking upstairs, you girls!" said Mrs. Corrie, kissing them good-night; and, though her smile was quite pleasant, it was always quite firm.

"Ten minutes, Mother?" Maggie pleaded.

"Ten minutes that really *is* ten minutes, Maggie," said Mrs. Corrie.

Upstairs in Joan's bedroom, Maggie's tongue ran as if she meant to make the very most of her brief interval. Did Joan swim? Oh, good! Then they would go to the Baths in the morning. And she played tennis, of course? Then that would do for the afternoon. And—oh, bother! Her watch had stopped—did Joan know the time?

"Why, what a funny place to wear a watch! And what a tiny little thing!" she exclaimed, as Joan looked at her wrist before answering. (She, for her part, though she hadn't said so, had thought it far funnier to wear a watch, as Maggie did, in a queer little patch-pocket stitched on to the front of her dress, with a watch-chain attached that was fastened through a buttonhole.)

"I had it last Christmas," seemed a harmless and non-committal answer.

"Why, so did I have mine! And I was most frightfully disappointed, when I opened the box on Christmas morning, because I thought I'd never had a watch-pocket and I wouldn't be able to wear it that day; and what do you think? Mother had waited till I was asleep, and then fetched my dress and stitched the pocket on!"

"How very nice," said Joan politely.

"But yours is so tiny," Maggie repeated. "I've never seen one so small! I'm afraid you will never be able to keep it in the watch-pocket on the bed."

She was looking—and Joan looked too—at a singular contrivance that she had not previously noticed: a sort of heavy rosette on the curtain at the bed's head, with a large gilt hook fixed in the middle of it.

"Oh, I'll manage," she said, again politely.

"And now I'm afraid our ten minutes are up, and I must go," said Maggie, ruefully, but with a most meritorious obedience. She kissed Joan heartily—a surprising thing to do—and ran off to her own room next door. And Joan instantly seized the opportunity to do what she had been longing to do, though she hadn't liked to do it before: to throw open the tightly closed window, top and bottom, and put her head out into the fresh and sweet sea-air. ... What a *shame* to have spent all this lovely evening indoors! And how queer to be sent off to bed at eight, as if she were a child—though, as a matter of fact, it was surprisingly dark for such an early hour, at this time of year. ... Perhaps Slonsea (which seemed to be a singularly old-fashioned place) hadn't yet heard of Summer Time!

She undressed, and put on, with much distaste, the long

heavy cotton night-gown that Maggie had brought her. It trailed on the ground—and yet she was only an inch or so the shorter of the two girls. It was high to the throat, with a frill of heavy embroidery, and a deep sailor-collar behind, trimmed with the same embroidery; and so were the tight cuffs of the long sleeves. It was tucked and embroidered half-way down the front, and it fastened with linen buttons. ... And Joan had worn nothing but pyjamas at night, since before she went to school.

She was contemplating herself in the glass, and thinking what a figure of fun she looked, when a tap at the door heralded the entrance of Mrs. Corrie.

"I just looked in to see that you have all you want, Joan. ... My *dear!*"

She was at the window, shutting it with quick, decided fingers.

"How exceedingly careless of Sarah! She is a little upset to-night and she must have forgotten. I will speak to her about it to-morrow. What a good thing I came in!"

"Please don't scold Sarah," Joan murmured awkwardly. "It wasn't her fault—the window *was* shut. I opened it myself."

"You should not have done that," Mrs. Corrie answered, with gravity. "Of course, I know that it has been very warm to-day; but surely your mother has taught you that night-air is dangerous?"

Joan hung her head, in what had all the appearance of being a very guilty manner. She didn't see her way to answering both politely and truthfully: since Mrs. Partridge's theory had always been that the most dangerous thing in the world was a stuffy room.

"I was sure she must have done so," said Mrs. Corrie, taking agreement as a matter of course. "And of course you meant, naturally, to shut it again before you got into bed. But I know what you girls are, when you get excited together!"

She smiled very kindly, and kissed Joan again: going on talking for a minute more, obviously just to show that there was no ill-feeling.

"I sent a line to your headmistress, to say that you had arrived safely. ... I wonder if you still find it difficult—Maggie and I still do!—to remember to put the right year?"

The right year. ... Joan stared at her, in a hopeless fog.

"One had grown so accustomed to the eighties, for such a long time. I find it hard to remember that this is eighteen-ninety! ... Good-night, my dear."

She was gone: leaving Joan standing stupefied in the middle of the room, wearing Maggie's long night-gown, staring, without seeing it, at the tightly-shut window.

CHAPTER VI

FORTY YEARS BACK

SUCH a terrific shock might have been expected to give Joan a sleepless night; but it did not—perhaps it merely stunned her. She certainly found herself murmuring in a dazed fashion to herself, as she got into bed: "Eighteen-ninety! Eighteen-ninety!" But it was all too confusing, and her evening's experiences had already been enough to puzzle and tire her head pretty completely. She found her eyes closing heavily; and the next thing she was sure of was the entrance of Sarah the housemaid, brisk and neat in her big cap and plain apron and a very pretty blue print frock (down to her heels, of course), saying that it was half-past seven and a lovely morning. She drew back the heavy reddish curtains without opening the window: put hot water in a basin; and departed. Joan's first action was to leap out of bed—very nearly tripping up over her long nightgown—and throw that window wide open. Even Mrs. Corrie couldn't object to morning air coming in! and it was most deliciously sweet fresh morning air, with a salt tang to it. Joan's head, which had been aching a little, cleared up as if by magic.

The deserted Square, so early in the day, looked just as it might in the nineteen-thirties. The sea, of course, looked as the sea always does look and presumably always will: blue to-day, with little brisk wavelets running up the beach, for the tide was nearly full. The very few people visible on the parade were too far off to be anything but just *people*. Joan found herself cheering up every moment, and inclined to laugh at what must have been a rather absurd dream. True, the nightgown was quite tangible; but then Mrs. Corrie was evidently very old-fashioned—which would account also for Sarah's uniform. She was also, obviously, very strict, and it would never do to be late for breakfast. Joan turned briskly. ...

And stood planted, with her mouth a little open and her eyes growing rounder and rounder.

St. Aldate's was particular about the tidiness of bedrooms, and girls very quickly learned to put things in their places and keep them there. Joan had arranged her clothes neatly, as she took them off, on the chair at the foot of her bed, hanging her drill-slip and blouse on the back of it. They were not there. The chair certainly held clothes—but not her clothes! Oh, no! They couldn't, Joan told herself in a fascination of horror, be intended for *her* to wear.

She took up the first in a very gingerly fashion. It was in perfectly good condition, but certainly not new. Very kind of Maggie, of course, to have lent her these things. ...

Joan stood still again, with another little gasp; for the mark, immediately under her thumb, was quite unmistakable— "J. R. Partridge" in marking-ink: not even the woven name-tape which was obligatory at St. Aldate's, but marked on the material. It was a little faded, as if with several washings. It certainly hadn't been done last night—even if Mrs. Corrie had known her second initial, which was most unlikely. Miss Crewe would have written of her, of course, just as Joan Partridge; and Mrs. Corrie must have been a magician if she guessed that R. stood for Rosemary.

The clock in the hall—a large grandfather, which she had noticed on her way up to bed—boomed out eight stately strokes; and Joan jumped. She mustn't, whatever she did, be late for breakfast! She must put on these incredible garments, and—and find out where her own were, as soon as she got downstairs. She told herself this very bravely, though with a sinking heart: which knew, at the bottom of it, that these *were* her clothes. In some incomprehensible fashion, she had been translated more than forty years back from her own time, and her clothes, as soon as she took them off, had—had returned, presumably, to the nineteen-thirties. Joan wished, with every wishing-power that was in her, that she could do the same.

She found the things most complicated, fussy, and tiresome—and so many of them! Everything fastened with hooks or buttons, and she was not accustomed to either. When it came to the question of stays, Joan held up that heavy, well-boned atrocity, and almost gave up her efforts. How on earth did one fasten the thing? By the time she had got half-way down the fastenings, the top had come undone and pinched her; if she started at the bottom, she couldn't do the top at all. When, at long last, she got it all done, she stood and panted. It was so tight! It made her look such a funny shape! It prevented her from breathing as she was accustomed to breathe, or moving freely as she was accustomed to move. And, even so, she wasn't at the end; for there was still a plain cotton garment, like the lining that a new dressmaker makes at her first fitting, and apparently it went on over the stays and buttoned down tight in front. Joan gave a gasp, and considered herself in the glass. She was decidedly flushed after her struggles, and her forehead was unbecomingly damp.

The grandfather clock struck the quarter. She must hurry indeed, for she would certainly have to wash her face again, if she wished to go downstairs looking decent. She took from the back of the chair the queer, long, cotton frock, very much trimmed, high to the neck, coming down to her ankles, fastening in the front with buttons—and it suddenly occurred to her that, for some reason, she hadn't yet put her stockings on. They were black cotton stockings, thick and long; and the awful stays had no suspenders attached, and Joan could see no garters anywhere. Luckily, she knew how to twist her stockings under her knees. ...

She was still occupied thus, when a knock at the door, being answered, produced Maggie: cheerful and eager and full of chat. Joan, feeling inordinately conspicuous and unnatural, found herself getting hot again, hardly liking to look at her; but a furtive glance was reassuring. Maggie, apparently, didn't see anything that wasn't as it should be, and wasn't in the least surprised to find her visitor dressed as she was herself. She seemed to take it as quite the natural thing.

"Why, did you lose your garters?" she cried, suddenly; and dived under the chair, and produced two rings of plain elastic, which Joan had seen and ignored. She said: "Oh, thank you!" in a blank voice, and put them on.

"Mother doesn't approve of elastic; she says it is bad for one's legs," Maggie informed her cheerfully. "Look, this is what I wear!"

She displayed an extraordinary wisp of wool, several strands thick, which she wore twisted round her leg just under the knee, and then tucked into itself.

"I'll make you some, if you like," she offered kindly. "They're ever so much more comfortable than elastic! and no trouble at all, when you once get the trick of twisting them at the right tightness."

"Thank you," said Joan blankly, in a muffled voice; she had put the cotton frock over her head, since that seemed the only way of getting into it, and was now entangled in its ample folds. Maggie lent a friendly hand, and extricated her, and helped to do up the many buttons in front.

"I always put on my boots when I get up; it saves time afterwards, if we want to go out at once," she suggested; and helpfully brought a pair of high black button-boots, which were standing under the wash-stand, and even offered to do up the buttons, which she accomplished very quickly and skilfully—much more so than Joan could possibly have done.

She *had* worn boots of course, for skating and hockey and so on—but not in the least like these, and never on a hot summer morning.

"Ready?" Maggie inquired cheerfully; and led the way downstairs. Joan, following, had never felt so uncomfortable in her life, or so conspicuous. The stays irked her, every time she breathed; the lace frill at her throat was starched quite stiff; the boots already made her feet feel hot and swollen. But Mrs. Corrie, looking at her kindly (and, of course, kissing her), appeared to find everything quite all right. It was obvious that she had had nothing to do with supplying these hateful clothes; she just took their appearance as a matter of course. She was glad to hear that Joan had slept well. She was glad that it was such a lovely day. She began to pour out tea; and Joan found herself eating bread-and-milk (which she had always hated) out of a bowl.

"I hope they give you bread-and-milk in the summer at St. Aldate's, and don't keep on with porridge too long?" said Mrs. Corrie.

Joan said No, they—they didn't have bread-and-milk; and Mrs. Corrie was quite grieved about it. She said that porridge was much too heating for this sort of weather; she was not at all sure that she should not write about it—and, meanwhile, Joan thought wistfully of the breakfast-table at St. Aldate's, surrounded by fortunate girls in drill-slips and thin cotton blouses with short sleeves. No, certainly not bread-and-milk! Force, and grape-nuts, and all that sort of thing; and plenty of fruit, according to the time of year, to finish up with— St. Aldate's prided itself extremely upon the amount of fruit given to the girls. There was none on this table. There were boiled eggs, and of course bread and toast, and butter and jam and marmalade. It all tasted very *good*; Joan was forced to confess this, when she had got through the bread-and-milk and gone on to an egg. She had never eaten such good bread, or such delicious butter; and the jam and marmalade, evidently home-made, were both excellent.

"Now," said Mrs. Corrie, as they rose from the table, "I am letting Maggie off all but half-an-hour of her practising to-day, for a holiday treat; but that she must do, and she had better do it at once. What about you, Joan? I shall be busy with housekeeping. I expect you would like to write to your mother."

"Thank you," said Joan; and hoped that her voice did not sound too faint. ... How *could* she write to her mother? How could any letter go from one century to another? and, apart from that, in eighteen-ninety her mother wouldn't have *been* her mother, but a baby of less than a year old! She couldn't explain this in any way, of course. She could only accept a pen and an ink-pot, and envelopes, and some double sheets of plain paper, and a strange mauve stamp with Queen Victoria's head upon it. If anything had been necessary to bring home to her the strangeness of her position, that stamp would have done it most effectually. And, driven by necessity, she did a most deceitful thing, which would have horrified Mrs. Corrie if she had known; she enclosed a blank sheet of paper in the envelope, and addressed it to the London address where, of course, her mother wasn't now living at all (since she was still a small baby in her father's house in Shropshire), and stuck on the unfamiliar stamp, and left the letter (that wasn't a letter) lying on a table in the hall. She had had some idea of running out to the post with it; but refrained, remembering what had befallen Sarah last night. Perhaps such a proceeding would be just as improper for a guest, staying in the house, as for a servant.

"Done!" cried Maggie thankfully, coming out of the drawing-room: from which, for a solid conscientious half-hour, had been heard sad sounds of scales and finger-exercises, with a good many mistakes in them.

"Are we going out now?" Joan inquired.

"Well, presently. But Mother doesn't allow us to bathe for two hours after a meal, of course; and Effie is coming this morning, and I do so want you to see her."

Effie, it appeared, was Maggie's elder sister, married last year to a Slonsea doctor; and she was quite evidently a great heroine. Maggie displayed the wedding group with enormous pride; and Joan, gazing at dresses that seemed to her perfectly hideous, found it difficult to comment adequately.

"Our frocks *were* pretty—well, you'll see mine to-morrow," said Maggie, the proud ex-bridesmaid.

"What colour were they?" Joan inquired; the only harmless question that occurred to her.

"Peacock-blue," said Maggie.

They were frocks with long tight sleeves, down to the wrist, oddly puckered at the shoulder. The bodice—buttoned of course all down the front—was clumsily drawn into a tight waist-belt, quite plain; the collar was of course high, with a lace frill. The skirt was obviously made of a great quantity of stuff, but it was drawn and gathered and bunched until it looked rather tight than otherwise.

"It was the first time I had a real bustle!" said Maggie.

"A real *what?*" said Joan.

"Haven't you had a bustle yet?" said Maggie, always kind, but obviously feeling superior.

"No," said Joan.

"Oh, well, I'll show you now!" said Maggie. "Come up to my room and see."

It was the first time that Joan had been there, and she looked round with interest—a very bare room, was her first impression, just like the spare room where she herself was sleeping. There was no book-shelf, no table, no comfortable chair. The dressing-table was also draped in muslin, with blue shiny stuff under it, like the pink shiny stuff in Joan's room.

The only thing that made it look like a girl's room, in Joan's eyes, was the row of little ornaments on the mantel-shelf: china animals, of all shapes and sizes. Maggie coloured a little, seeing them observed.

"I'm afraid they do look rather babyish," she confessed. "But I've collected them for such a long time—ever since I was quite small. And you have to collect *something*."

Joan agreed: thinking of cigarette cards, and photographs of film heroes, and foreign stamps, and (by one young lady who had money to burn) gramophone records.

"What do you collect?" Maggie inquired.

"Pictures of aeroplanes," said Joan; and said it rather proudly, for it was surely quite a sensible collection to make—more like a boy's than a girl's. But Maggie only stared at her, asking, in a dazed tone, *what* she had said. And, when Joan repeated it, she was obviously none the wiser. ... Of course she wasn't. This was eighteen-ninety, any number of years before the first flying-machine flew. ... Joan felt a little cold chill, to which, by this time, she was becoming quite accustomed. It wasn't, of course, any *use* trying to explain. ... What a mercy that Maggie, who really was an extremely nice girl, didn't press the question that was evidently inexplicable and embarrassing.

"I think," she was saying meditatively, "that I really must begin to make some other collection for next term—it's a good time to begin, after the summer, don't you think? Perhaps you could suggest something new?"

Joan shook her head; but she was not really thinking of Maggie's question at all. She was thinking, with another cold shiver, that what she herself would have meant by "next term" was more than forty years away—and that Miss Crewe, at the present moment, could be only two years old!

"Here's my frock," said Maggie, who had been busy at a long drawer. She laid the source of her pride on the bed; and her tone said that she was very proud of it indeed. Joan gazed in silence.

The frock, in her eyes, was extraordinarily hideous: not only the harsh, bright colour, but the tucks and ruffles and elaborate pleatings. Fingering it awkwardly, to gain a little time, she came upon something hard and flat.

"What's this?"

"Why, that's the bustle!" said Maggie, prouder than ever.

It was stitched in at the back of the waist, just under where the skirt fastened with hooks and eyes; and it was a thick, hard little pad, apparently filled with something stiff and unyielding.

"What *is* it made of?"

"Horsehair, of course!" said Maggie, surprised at the question.

"But what's it *for?*"

"Why, to make the skirt stand out well, of course!" said Maggie, staring at her. "*All* grown-up people wear them— *much* bigger than this! Doesn't your mother—but of course she does!"

It was equally impossible for Joan to say Yes or No; one answer was, naturally, untrue, and the other would obviously be quite incredible to Maggie. As a matter of fact, a sudden vision of her pretty graceful mother, in the delightful clothes that she wore so beautifully, made speech impossible for the moment. Not quite sure whether she was going to burst into tears or laughter, Joan went on staring with absorption at the frock, as the safest course to take.

"I should think the—the bustle must be very hot and heavy," she remarked at last.

Maggie agreed at once.

"Oh, yes, it is. But it does make a skirt sit most beautifully!"

Joan had heard of people suffering to be beautiful; but this, in her eyes, was suffering to be hideous. Since she couldn't say so, and couldn't think of anything more polite, words failed her again; and she was heartily relieved when a sound of horse-hoofs under the window made Maggie fly to look out, crying gladly:

"Oh, here's Effie!"

CHAPTER VII

SHINGLE AND SHINGLING

JOAN went quickly enough to the window also, curious to see the heroine. A carriage stood at the door, very smart, with a fine bay horse and a coachman in a blue livery—a very queer carriage in Joan's eyes, which had never seen anything like it before. But that was not what made her stare so.

"Maggie, *how* old did you say your sister was?"

"Nineteen," said Maggie proudly. "She was only eighteen when she was married!"

"But ... but she's wearing a *bonnet!*"

"Well, of course! for driving," said Maggie, staring in her turn. "Married women always *do*. It has nothing to do with age."

Her tone said, plainly enough, two things: that it was a very fine feat to be married at eighteen; and that all single women must be eaten up with envy because they were not counted worthy to wear bonnets if they wished.

They ran downstairs. The front door was open, and Mrs. Corrie was in the hall, kissing the newcomer: upon whom Maggie also flew instantly with caresses. But, always polite and kind, she remembered her guest the next moment: "Oh, Effie, this is Joan Partridge, who is staying with us!"

"How jolly for you, Maggie!" said the bonnet-wearer, in a fresh, gay young voice, shaking hands with Joan as if not quite sure that she ought not to kiss her also. ... Yes; it *was* a very young face under the bonnet: which was a definite bonnet, tied under the chin with black velvet strings, but otherwise very small and jaunty, with a rose in it. She wore the most bunchy dress that Joan had yet seen, sticking out behind in the most extraordinary way—a bustle underneath, Joan knew now at once; and a queer little fussy coat, that came just below her waist and there stuck out very much too, because it couldn't help it.

"Ready, Mother dear?"

"I was just going up to dress when you came. Talk to the girls for a minute," said Mrs. Corrie, with her hand on the banister.

The chattering of Maggie and Effie left no need for Joan to say anything: she just absorbed and wondered. Though Effie looked young, she *seemed* old—much older than any girl of nineteen whom Joan had ever known. She talked, not of driving and dancing and tennis, but of her house and her garden and her husband, of whom she was evidently very fond and proud. She listened with great interest to all that Maggie rattled off about games and school; but it was a completely detached interest, as if she had left all that far behind. It seemed as if, when she married, she had given up everything that is usually attractive to a girl of nineteen, and become quite a different person.

"Going to the Baths? Yes, how jolly!" (But no suggestion that she might join them there, when she had taken her mother for the promised drive.)

"Yes, it must have been perfect weather for tennis, this last week." (No intimation that she herself had been playing, or had wished to play.)

"Yes, I always hated quadrilles myself! … Oh, here you are, Mother dear! Let us start at once; for I promised Horace to fetch him from the Hospital at one."

They took their seats in the very strange carriage; which was low and had only two seats, very comfortable-looking. It was quite open, and the door at each side was so low that a long-legged person could easily have stepped over it. The coachman tucked them in carefully with a light striped cotton rug, to keep off dust; and each of them put up a large sunshade with a deep lace frill—Mrs. Corrie's black with a white lining, Effie's tussore lined with pink, which threw a charming rosy glow over her pretty face. Mrs. Corrie was of course wearing a bonnet, large and impressive, though it had a little white lace in it to relieve the black; and she wore a curious short black mantle, fussy and lacy, coming down over her arms and then opening into slits through which her hands appeared, in black kid gloves. But Joan, having once noticed her boots, found everything else unimportant: black boots, of course, with no fastening at all, but an inset of black elastic at each side. ... It has not been mentioned, by the way, that both the carriage-folk wore veils, drawn tightly down over their faces, and fastened by some invisible agency under their chins. Mrs. Corrie's was of a plain coarse net; but Effie's had large black chenille spots at intervals, which, Joan thought, must be very bad for her eyes.

"Good-bye, dears," said Mrs. Corrie, smiling at them as the coachman flicked his horse lightly, and they started off. "Remember, only twenty minutes!"

"Twenty minutes *what?*" Joan inquired.

"Twenty minutes in the water, when we bathe."

"But ... why?" Joan asked again, much taken aback.

"Well, it's not good to stay in too long, of course," said Maggie, surprised. "How long are *you* allowed to stay in?"

"Well—any time," said Joan vaguely. "We just get into our bathing-dresses and *stay* in them."

"And go in and out of the water as you please?"

"Yes, of course!"

"But that is the sea, of course—not Baths?"

"Yes," said Joan.

"Of course that makes it a *little* different," said Maggie, obviously disapproving. "But what do you *do* all the time? It must be very dull in the bathing-machines!"

"Bathing-machines?" Joan repeated.

"Where you change," Maggie explained, a little as if she was teaching A.B.C. to a very dull child.

"We change in tents: or sometimes just behind rocks."

"Behind *rocks!*" Maggie exclaimed, in a terribly shocked voice.

"Why not?" said Joan, becoming a little restive.

"*Well!*" said Maggie, as if the answer were so obvious that she saw no need to give it. Then, relenting, she added kindly: "But of course it must be some very lonely place."

"It needn't be," said Joan, still restive. "We went to Aberystwyth last year, when we were staying with my grandfather in Shropshire just drove over for the day; and that is quite a biggish place. It was very hot; and we were in our bathing-dresses nearly all the time—it was the only thing to do, to keep comfortable."

"But you couldn't stay in the sea all day!"

"Of course not. We came out and sat on the sands, and then went in again when we felt like it."

"*You sat on the sands!*" said Maggie, in a low voice of horror. "In your *bathing-dresses!*"

"Of course we did!" said Joan. "Why not?"

Perhaps Maggie couldn't answer that; at any rate, she didn't. As if feeling it wise to change the subject, she said after a minute, in a repressed voice:

"I thought Aberystwyth was in Wales?"

"So it is: the west coast."

"But—you said you were staying in *Shropshire?*"

"So we were."

"But—you said you *drove* over?"

"So we did."

"For the *day!*"

Joan nodded impatiently. She really thought Maggie extremely dense.

"But—isn't it a long way?"

"Yes, rather—seventy or eighty miles, I suppose. We weren't back till nearly nine o'clock."

"Does your grandfather live a long way from a station?"

"Yes—five or six miles."

"Oh, I see!" said Maggie, evidently much relieved. "You mean that you were driven to the station, and then met when you came back!"

It wasn't in the least what Joan had meant; but she suddenly realised that she had better leave it at that. ... Of course Maggie had never seen a car, or any kind of motor, because there weren't any!

"It must have been great fun," said Maggie, in her kind way. "How many of you went?"

"Oh, about a dozen! There were several cousins staying at my grandfather's, and the people from the Hall, and three of the Vicarage boys."

"*Boys!*" said Maggie, in the strangest tone.

"Well, they're really more than that: only we've always known them, and they're always called the Vicarage boys," said Joan. "Archie is twenty, and the twins nearly eighteen."

"But—*boys!*" said Maggie, in exactly the same voice.

"Well! why not?" said Joan, becoming restive again.

"How *did* you manage about the bathing?"

"Why, we all bathed together, of course!" said Joan blankly. (Really, Maggie was extraordinarily stupid. What did she expect them to have done?)

The answer had an extraordinary effect. Maggie gasped a little, and stared. Then she said, quite severely (for anyone so kind and polite):

"How *could* your chaperon allow it?"

"My *what?*"

"Your chaperon?"

"I'm afraid I don't know what you mean," said Joan, also

puzzled, but also polite. "What *is* a—what you said?"

"Why, whoever went with you!" Maggie cried, in quite an outraged voice. "Your mother, or—or whoever it was!"

"Mummy didn't go; she isn't strong, and doesn't like motoring far," said Joan. ... The word slipped out before she was aware; however, Maggie was far too perturbed to notice it.

"But *some* grown-up person went?" she cried, almost shrilly.

"No," said Joan. "Why should they? We could all swim; and everybody over seventeen had a driving-licence."

"A *what?*"

"A driving-licence."

Maggie gave it up as a bad job.

"And your mother *let* you go?" she said, in a hushed voice.

"Of course," said Joan. "It was quite safe; and she isn't nervous, as long as she knows the drivers are all right."

Maggie's astounded face conveyed, quite clearly, that she thought Joan must have a most remarkable mother.

"I knew it was sometimes done abroad. I didn't think it was done *anywhere* in England!" she said.

"What?" said Joan.

"Why, people bathing—together—like that."

Joan held her tongue: with a little difficulty, but she creditably held it. She, for her part, knew—from *Punch*, and so on—that there were still places where Mayors and people were fussy about this sort of thing. Evidently the Mayor of Slonsea must be one of the fussy ones.

"Are we going now?" she asked amiably.

"Yes," said Maggie, in a subdued voice. "We'd better start. I didn't see how the time had got on."

She was still evidently very much scandalised and upset; and Joan also felt that she had something of a grievance, which swelled to vexation as she went upstairs to fetch the stiff sailor hat, hanging on the door. ... How *did* the rotten thing stick on? It perched uncomfortably on the very top of her head, and would, obviously, fly off at the first breath of sea-breeze. She eventually found an elastic loop behind, which went under her hair and looked hideous. Maggie's, of course—Joan had a good look, when they met in the hall—was hidden underneath her long hair, and only showed a little at the sides.

"What a pity you forgot to bring your bathing-dress! But they have quite nice ones for hire at the Baths," said Maggie. "I always leave mine there, because I go so often. … Did you bring down your towel? Oh, I'll run up and get it for you … and shall I fetch your gloves too?"

"We don't *need* gloves, do we?" said Joan ruefully. But Maggie looked really shocked.

"Oh, yes, of *course*—for going on the front, you know! I won't be a minute. …"

She ran down again with the towel, and a very thick clumsy pair of brown kid gloves, hot and ugly, which Joan put on with an added ruefulness. *Gloves!* on a hot July morning, by the seaside, with a cotton frock. But Maggie's manner showed quite clearly that there was no appeal, and she was wearing exactly the same kind herself. They set out.

"I do hope some of the girls will be there to meet us. I asked them to," said Maggie, a little anxiously.

"Don't you ever go in the sea?" Joan asked.

"No, not often. The bathing-boxes are so stuffy and sandy—and sometimes not even clean. Besides, I can't bother Mother to go very often; she doesn't like bathing."

"But you could go alone, couldn't you?"

"Oh, *no!*" said Maggie, so freshly scandalised that Joan didn't like to ask why not. Instead, as they walked along the Parade, she stared with interest at the machines down on the beach, like little Noah's arks on wheels, with very aged horses, and men to drive them. She saw, a little, why Maggie had been so thunder-struck at the idea of mixed bathing; for here there were two distinct groups of bathing-machines, discreetly separated by quite a large expanse of beach, and labelled, very largely and clearly, Ladies and Gentlemen. It appeared that one went up into the machine by a flight of wooden steps, and down into the sea on the other side by another flight! in between, the man harnessed the horse in front, and dragged the whole thing down a little way into the water, and then unharnessed the horse and took him back to the beach. No one seemed to move far from the machine, or to do anything very exciting. Some people swam, rather timidly, close in shore: others merely bobbed up and down in an aimless manner, occasionally splashing each other and screaming, holding a rope that was fastened to the machine. When they had bathed for as long as they thought proper—a very little time seemed usually enough—they scrambled up the seaward steps with extreme haste and nervousness, and disappeared inside; and the horse was harnessed again, this time on the landward side, and dragged the machine once more up the beach to where it had been before. It all looked the dullest thing in the world. There was not a single person in a bathing-dress visible on the beach: though one or two girls sat, fully dressed, and dried their long hair in the sunshine.

"Isn't your hair an awful bother to dry? Doesn't the water get up under your cap?" Joan inquired.

"I don't generally wear a cap. They are so uncomfortable; and my hair gets wet anyhow," said Maggie.

"Why don't you have it shingled?"

"Have it *what?*" said Maggie: after a puzzled glance at the shingle on the beach, as if the word conveyed nothing else to her.

"Well—like mine!"

"But you had yours cut because you were ill, I suppose?"

"Oh, *no*, I didn't!" said Joan, rather annoyed; for she had always been to a rather grand shop in London, where they did hair just as it ought to be done.

"Oh!" said Maggie: obviously in another of her polite dilemmas. She began to say something else; and then stammered, and checked herself hurriedly, and finally got out of the difficulty by saying that "Mother liked long hair." And it speedily became apparent to Joan that other people's mothers shared this odd and unfashionable taste; for, walking along the sea-front, they met pigtails, and hair tied back like Maggie's, and curls not tied at all, and quite young-looking girls with their hair done up, round and round at the back, under their sailor-hats, like very wide Chelsea buns. This seemed so surprising to Joan, that she remarked on it.

"Isn't she awfully *young*, to have her hair done like that?" she asked of a girl to whom Maggie had nodded.

"Well, she's only sixteen; but then she's so tall—it would look queer if she had it down."

"How she must hate it!" said Joan feelingly. But Maggie looked greatly surprised.

"Oh, *no!* Why should she? It must be great fun to put your hair up—but Mother wants me to wait till I'm seventeen."

She spoke of this as if she had to wait for a promised treat.

"Do you *want* to?" Joan asked bluntly.

"Why, of course I do! Don't you want to ..." Maggie trailed off awkwardly, after a glance at the back of Joan's head, and then picked up her speech and went on swimmingly ... "to leave school, and come out, and go to parties, and have fun?"

Joan, who already went to parties, and had as much fun as any girl had a right to expect, was fogged in her turn.

"Don't you go to any grown-up things now?"

"Why, of *course* not!" said Maggie, scandalised for yet another time. "At Effie's dance, I was allowed to come in for the first bit: but of course only in a high frock, and till ten o'clock—and only because it was in our own house!"

CHAPTER VIII

The Baths

"LOOK!" Maggie suddenly cried, with excitement. "There's Dr. Emery's car! Did you ever see one?" Joan's attention had been entirely turned to the beach. She looked now to the road, with quite a thrill—it would be really comforting to see something to which she was accustomed. She went on looking; and her face grew blank.

"Where?" she asked.

"Why, there! Just going to stop at the house with the pillars!"

Drawing up at the house with the pillars there was a carriage such as Joan had never seen before: on two wheels, with a seat each side—like a wagonette turned inside out, so that the people on each side would have their backs against each other. The driver sat on a little box-seat in front; and the whole thing was very smart and light and new, with a lively-looking bay cob in the shafts. But ...

"But that's not a *car!*" said Joan, her voice as blank as her face.

"Oh, yes, it is! an Irish jaunting-car," said Maggie. "Isn't it a jolly name? and it's simply spiffing to drive in! We know the Emerys; and I've been out in it twice—awfully difficult to hold on, if there's a sharp corner! Mrs. Emery is Irish, and he got it to please her."

"I ... see," said Joan slowly. And indeed she did. She saw, more clearly than ever, that she was a stranger in a strange land, where they didn't even mean the same things by the same words. ... And—*spiffing!* What an extraordinary term of praise! She had never heard it before in her life.

Her attention being turned in that direction, she saw also

how very different the traffic was from anything that she had ever seen before; in fact, what there was, was hardly worthy of the name. It was all, of course, horse-drawn: carts: carriages, some like the one in which Mrs. Corrie and Effie were driving, some like an open cab, some like a small closed car: buses, smaller than those which she knew, with two large horses, and a driver perched upon a seat above them. There were a few little carts drawn by donkeys. There were goat-chaises, waiting to be hired by very small children, drawn up by the railings. There were bicycles ...

There was something odd about the bicycles. One was leaning up against the railings; and Joan went closer to look at it.

"How on *earth* do you blow up your tyres?" she asked.

"How do I do *what?*" Maggie inquired, bewildered.

"Blow up your tyres. There's no valve."

"I don't know what you mean," said Maggie, speaking blankly in her turn. "They're just—india-rubber. How could they be blown up?"

They were, in fact, mere india-rubber tubes, like a gas-pipe.

"How queer!" said Joan, pinching one.

"They're quite new: they say they are a *great* improvement on the solid ones!" said Maggie, rather affronted.

"But what happens if you puncture?"

"If you *what?*"

"Puncture. Get a hole in them—a thorn, or a sharp stone."

"I don't believe they ever do," said Maggie.

"But you must *know*," Joan persisted. "Don't you ever get a puncture, yourself?"

"But ... *I* don't ride a bicycle, of course! Only men do," said Maggie, appalled.

"But that *is* a lady's bicycle!" Joan persisted.

"It can't be. There isn't such a thing!"

"But where's the diamond frame? Where's the crossbar?"

"I don't know *what* you mean," said Maggie; and they might have gone on for ever at cross-purposes, if the owner of the bicycle had not at that moment arrived, looked at them with dark suspicion, mounted—by the pedal—and ridden off. He was a tall young man with a moustache, a flannel blazer, and a straw hat.

They walked on; and Joan, silenced for the moment, looked attentively at the road and saw that Maggie was, incredibly, quite right. All the bicycles were like the one that she had examined; and they were all ridden by men or boys. They had an easy time of it, threading in and out of the slow wheeled traffic that looked, to Joan's eyes, so scanty. Anybody could cross the road anywhere, almost without troubling to look either way. … How very hot she felt, in her long clumsy frock, and her high black boots, and her thick kid gloves! and how unpleasantly her hat wobbled about, in spite of the elastic, whenever there came a little puff of sea-breeze.

"Those are some of our girls, riding," said Maggie.

They were riding with an elderly master, all very prim and proper, heads up and shoulders down. They wore short, full skirts, just covering their feet, and tight-fitting coat-bodices to match, with linen collars like a man's. They all wore bowler-hats, also like a man's. They all rode sidesaddle. … It seemed likely to shock Maggie afresh if one inquired whether no one rode astride; so Joan didn't ask it. Most of the girls looked very hot. Each of them carried, bunched up with the reins, a little neat riding-switch.

"And *those* are two of our girls, on in front," said Maggie. "Mildred Ayres and Eva Dugan. They're tremendous chums, always together: they always dance together at break—very fast! They can waltz double-time; and everyone gets out of the way, I can tell you. You see, Mildred is as quick as lightning, and Eva is very big!"

The girls in question had been stopped by two other girls,

in the inevitable sailor-hats; and Joan looked at them with
interest. One was very dark, slim, and lithe, with an immense
pigtail of black hair; the other was much taller, much broader,
much fairer, with quantities of hair plaited round and round at
the back of her head, like basket-work.

"Come along!" said Maggie, suddenly in a hurry. "I don't
want to meet those two."

"What's the matter with them?" Joan asked curiously.

"No, no—not Mildred and Eva. They're all right—rather
queer, but all *right*. It's the others. ..."

As Maggie and Joan came up, the four girls in front were
parting company; and one of those coming their way was
saying, in a loud, affected voice: "Oh, Mildredayres" (all in
one word), "what a *funny* girl you are!" Joan looked, curiously
again, at the two who were supposed to be "not all right." The
thing that chiefly struck her was their shape, which was much
like that of an hour-glass; and, next after that, their hair. Each
wore her hat slightly tilted forward; and the hair underneath
was curled in quantities of tiny tight curls, coming down
almost to their eye-brows. Each carried a little light cane; and
their boots, though quite definitely boots, were thin and tight
and high-heeled.

"Hullo, Maggie!" said one of them, making as if to stop.
But the polite and kindly Maggie, quickening her pace a little,
merely said in a hurry: "Oh, hullo, Gladys—we're going to the
Baths!" and bore Joan away with her.

"What's the matter with *them?*"

Maggie, waiting till the people in question must be safely
out of hearing, replied in a low, impressive voice:

"Gladys Herries and Gertrude Bryce. They're *fast*. Don't
you *see?*" Maggie cast a half-glance over her shoulder. "Their
sticks, and their eyes, and their being so tight-laced, and their
fringes, and—oh, everything! Mother doesn't like them *at all*.
I'm very glad they aren't in my Form; and so is she."

"What *are* fringes?"

"Why, didn't you *see* their hair?"

Joan had; and it had reminded her strongly of Effie's coiffure—but obviously that was the very last comment to make. She waited, accordingly, for further information.

"Mother says it's horrid for girls to do their hair in Alexandra fringes before they're out."

"All those curls—is *that* an Alexandra fringe?"

"Yes, of course!"

"Why are they called that?"

"After the Princess of Wales, of course. *She* started the fashion."

"But there *isn't* ..."

Joan pulled herself up sharply, just in time; and history not being her strong point—tried frantically to remember about the Royal Family in eighteen-ninety. Queen Victoria was reigning, of course; and the Prince of Wales was—why, he was Edward the Seventh! Then the Princess, about whom Maggie was talking, must be Queen Alexandra; and, of course, her hair *had* been like that, when you came to think of it. ...

"Here we are!" said Maggie, beginning to go down steps into a sort of large paved well, with doors opening from it at either side: one saying Ladies and the other Gentlemen. Into Ladies, Maggie and Joan turned; and found themselves in a heated saltish atmosphere, with a very hot, stout woman in a sort of ticket-office, surrounded by pigeon-holes full of dry bathing-dresses and towels. Wet ones were, apparently, dropped at her feet as people went out; they lay there in heaps, looking very unappetising. Maggie's own was produced, and another for Joan; and they went upstairs, where it was less damp but even hotter, and took possession of two wooden cubicles side by side.

What a joy to get off that waggling hat, those boots, those tight and oppressive clothes! Joan drew long breaths of relief

as she laboriously freed herself from one after another; she
eyed vengefully the festoons of unwieldy garments, hung up
on one hook after another ... How different from the old
days—they seemed centuries ago by this time—when it had
been a matter of half a minute to slip out of two or three
garments and into ...

She took up the bathing-dress, and looked at it; and words
failed her.

It weighed, even when dry, quite an appreciable amount:
when wet, Joan thought it must be about half-a-ton. It was
made of solid thick blue serge—navy-blue—in two parts; and
each part was painstakingly trimmed with rows of red braid.
The knickers came well below her knees; the tunic was like a
dress, down to her knees, and finished off, behind at the top,
with a good square sailor-collar, outlined in red braid also. The
only looking-glass in the cubicle was about six inches square.
Joan was quite unable to get any glimpse in it of the general
effect; but she was extremely angry with the hot woman in
the office—who might at least have *looked* at her, and chosen
something that was more or less the right size!

"Are you nearly ready?" cried the voice of Maggie outside.
And Joan, drawing back the curtain to answer wrathfully that
she would never be ready in these garments, bit her words off
short, and merely stared. Maggie's dress—her own dress, not
anything chance and hired—was exactly the same, in length,
breadth, and everything else, except that it was trimmed with
white braid instead of red. And Joan, of course, looked, more
or less, as Maggie was looking now—except that one face
was full of pleasant expectation, and the other was black with
frowns.

"Do let's come down! It's so hot up here," said Maggie; and
Joan (because it was quite useless to say anything of any sort)
followed in silence down the wet wooden stairs.

It was a very good swimming-bath; she was obliged to own

that. It was large; at the deep end it was seven foot; it had a good spring-board for diving, and steps all round at convenient intervals, for getting in and out. Being Saturday, a good many people were in it already: some at the shallow end, where a tired-looking girl was giving swimming-lessons, not so many at the deep end. They all, without exception, wore exactly the same sort of bathing-dresses as Maggie and Joan, and a few wore bathing-caps as well, all exactly alike, as if they had drawn a black-and-white sponge-bag over their heads. One girl was swimming very elegantly and slowly about, with an immense quantity of yellow hair piled up, perfectly dry, on the top of her head; it was quite evident that her constant thought was the fear of wetting it.

"That's Maud Sherwell," Maggie murmured to Joan. "She's in the Sixth. ... No, she never wets it. It comes down to her knees when she lets it down. Once Ella Tybald—she's *awful*—dived quite close on purpose, and splashed her frightfully. There *was* a row."

"It can't be much fun, just to swim about like that," said Joan, watching.

"No. But it would take her hours and hours to get the salt out, and dry it," said Maggie. "Can you swim?"

"Oh, yes!" said Joan carelessly.

As a matter of fact, she could swim very well, and was extremely proud of it.

"Then we'll go into the deep end—if you're *sure* you are safe."

"Aren't you going to dive?" Joan inquired.

"No, I hate it. Are you?"

Joan, nodding, ran out on to the spring-board, and dived in very neatly. It made something of a sensation—very few people seemed to care about that way of entering the water; heads turned to watch in all directions, including the piled yellow head of Miss Maud Sherwell.

"You *do* do it well!" said Maggie, who had swum out from the steps to meet her.

"Oh, it's very easy—so low!" said Joan; and cast her eye on a high flight of steps beside the spring-board. "I'm going up there now."

"You're not going from the top?"

"Yes, of course! Why not?"

"Oh, do be careful!" Maggie implored, agitated with responsibility.

"It's all right," Joan laughed back at her, climbing the steps. … *Heavens*, what a weight the thick serge bathing-dress was, when she was once out of the water! It hung dripping round her, and clung to her legs, and was altogether perfectly beastly. But she took off very neatly, for all that, from the top of the steps, and dived in after her very best style, and came up, laughing, beside the anxious Maggie: who applauded in a generous and astonished manner that was most satisfactory. … After all there *were* advantages in living before one's proper time. A good many people seemed to be watching with interest, including the swimming teacher; and then they turned again to their own affairs, and swam decorously about, or dived faint-heartedly from the side, or ran along the spring-board and jumped in, with a resounding splash. No one seemed to be doing the American crawl, or any other form of fancy swimming; it was obviously Joan's day. She swam to the extreme end of the bath, close to the spring-board, and then turned and swam, her very fastest, in the best style of crawl, to the barrier that hedged off the shallow end.

To her amazement, she found herself greeted there by quite a little bevy of people—all strangers but Maggie—who had rushed to meet her.

"Oh, Joan, are you all right?" Maggie cried anxiously.

"Of course I'm all right!" said Joan, astonished and annoyed. "Why not?"

"Why! you were swimming with your face under water! You *did* frighten me."

"Well, of course," said Joan again. "How else can you do the crawl?"

"The *what?*"

"The American crawl."

The little knot of people began to melt away at that, and Joan heard them murmuring amongst themselves: "Oh, she's *American!*" as if that might explain anything. But the swimming teacher, who had by this time left her pupil and come up, had a word to say.

"You are a wonderfully fast swimmer," she told Joan. "It is a pity, if you don't mind my saying so, that you don't take a few lessons and learn a better style."

Joan stared at her, speechless. What *cheek!* She knew quite well that her style was good; she had been well taught, and she had a natural gift for swimming.

"You see, the whole point of good swimming is *quietness*—look at Miss Sherwell, and you will see what I mean."

Joan looked, very wrathful, at the stately yellow-haired person, swimming very slowly and with great dignity and without a sound, the water only slightly rippling around her.

"You must see the difference, I'm sure," said the swimming-teacher kindly. "You went very fast indeed—I've never seen anyone do a better pace—but you did splash terribly!"

"You can't help splashing, when you're doing the American crawl," said Joan, in a stifled voice.

"The *what?*" asked the swimming-teacher, like Maggie.

"The American crawl!"

"I have never heard of it," said the swimming-teacher in a final voice: but a little uneasily, too, for it was her business to keep up with the times and learn any innovations.

Joan faced her, at bay and very angry.

"I'm sorry I can't do any other new things," she said. "I

don't think, as a matter of fact, anybody does them now—the trudgeon stroke has gone *quite* out of fashion. I did do the scissors kick—you saw me!"

"We've had our twenty minutes: we must go and dress now," Maggie murmured uneasily in her ear; and she took her arm, and edged her away.

"Miss Davis, it is time for your lesson," said the swimming-teacher, turning in the opposite direction. Though her new pupil was any age, and fat, and most unpromising in appearance, her voice sounded very much relieved indeed.

CHAPTER IX

Countess and Creamery

"ARE you ready, Joan?" Maggie asked, in a patient voice, for the second time. She had been waiting outside the cubicles for some minutes. It was extremely hot; and people were coming rather fast, so that every cubicle was in demand.

"*No!*" Joan's voice came in answer, savagely, with a hint of tears.

"What's the matter? Can I do anything?"

"It's these *beastly* buttons and things. ..."

"May I come in?" said Maggie; and, as Joan didn't absolutely say No, she pushed back the curtain and entered. A forlorn figure confronted her, with eyes suspiciously red, and a flushed and angry face. It wore stays and a petticoat, and had evidently been contorting itself unsuccessfully over boot-buttons, of which three were fastened.

"Oh, didn't you bring your button-hook? I *am* sorry. Why didn't you ask for mine?" cried Maggie, producing a folding one from her pocket. "Here, let me do it!"

She knelt down on the damp floor, and did the buttoning quickly and efficiently, like a person who is well used to it.

"I can't stoop, in these foul stays," said Joan, in a voice that was half-way between temper and apology.

Maggie jumped a little at the adjective, which seemed new to her. But she only said, mildly:

"Haven't you been *used* to wearing stays?"

"No!"

"There *is* one girl in my Form whose mother has never let her wear them," said Maggie politely. "She's artistic, and goes in for Liberty clothes, and all that sort of thing—queer dull colours, and no shape. But she'll find it awfully awkward when she Comes Out, because her waist will be about thirty inches by that time; she's a big girl."

"Well, why not?" said Joan blankly.

"*Well!*" said Maggie, with an equal blankness; and they stared at each other.

"I'm afraid someone is waiting for this cubicle," said Maggie, recovering; and Joan began to fumble awkwardly with her white cotton bodice. Maggie's quick, accustomed fingers came again to the rescue.

"Why *do* you have so many buttons?" Joan asked crossly.

"Well, hooks bend so in the wash. ..."

"But why not snaps?"

"*Snaps?*" said Maggie, bewildered.

"And why not a Zip fastening for your frock?" said Joan, in a muffled voice, with hers over her head.

"What *is* a Zip fastening?"

"Oh—didn't you ever see one?" said Joan, recollecting herself once more, as she wrestled with hooks and buttons.

"No, never! I never *heard* of such a thing," said Maggie, coming to the rescue again. "What is it?"

Joan, finding herself totally incapable of explaining under the circumstances, didn't try. She hurried to put on her hat and adjust the elastic; she took her gloves in one hand, and her towel and wet bathing-dress in the other, and announced herself ready. ... How fresh the air felt, though it was hot, as they emerged from under the doorway labelled Ladies, and went up the steps to the Parade. Here Maggie paused, a little awkwardly.

"Shall we wait a minute, while you put on your gloves?"

"Oh, *must* I wear them? My hands are so hot and sticky!" Joan complained.

"I'm afraid it will look rather ... queer if you don't," said Maggie: in so shocked a tone that Joan complied, without further protest. ... *How* hot they were, and how uncomfortable! But she could not help owning, as she looked round her, that all other feminine hands were similarly covered. A few very tiny children were lucky enough to be bare-handed; but otherwise they seemed, in Joan's eyes, most unfortunate little creatures. They wore stiff starched cotton frocks, with high collars and the inevitable lace frill, and long sleeves; and their small feet were all encased in long black stockings and little button boots. Even the few babies, who were taking the air in their nurses' arms, were swallowed up in immensely long long-clothes, with heavy cloaks, and close-fitting bonnets heavily trimmed with ribbon, and thick veils over their little faces. Joan had a mad feeling that, if one investigated under the long-clothes, they would all be wearing black stockings and buttoned boots.

"Look!" Maggie cried suddenly, with excitement. "Oh, we *are* lucky! That's the Countess's carriage; and she must be in that shop, and she'll come out in a minute!"

She almost ran to the railings by the roadside, where already a little crowd, having made a similar discovery, was gathering.

"*What* Countess?" asked Joan blankly.

"Why, the Countess of Claridge! She's staying down here at the Alexandra Hotel. Have you ever seen her?"

Joan shook her head.

"Well, you know of course that she's a Famous Society Beauty," said Maggie, in hushed tones. "Her photographs are in *all* the windows; and she's perfectly lovely!"

Joan listened and looked round, amazed. The fast-gathering crowd, like Maggie, was thoroughly excited; they might have been expecting to see Royalty, or at least some famous film-star. And suddenly a little murmur ran from mouth to mouth, and Maggie murmured: "Look! look!" and a lady emerged from the shop, opposite, and looked round, pausing for a minute—she seemed quite accustomed to this sort of homage—and then stepped into the very smart carriage that was drawn up, waiting for her, smiling and bowing as if she had indeed been Royalty. She had beautiful dark eyes, and a quantity of hair done in an incredibly curled fringe down to her eyebrows, and she was not in the least made up ... so much Joan noticed; but otherwise she was lost in amazement at her general appearance. She was far from slim; but Joan could have clasped her waist in her two hands. Her clothes were trimmed, and frilled, and flounced, and bunched, wherever it was possible to do any of these things. Her black stockings were silk; her little black boots were pointed and high-heeled. She wore a sailor-hat, tilted smartly over her nose, and a veil over it, irregularly dotted with huge black spots. She put up a very fine lace sunshade, with a dangling frill of lace all round; and the liveried footman climbed to his seat beside the liveried coachman, who whipped up his fine pair of bay horses, and drove very smartly away. The crowd gave a little hoarse roar of applause, and an excitable lady waved a handkerchief.

"Isn't she *lovely!*" said Maggie reverentially, as they walked on again.

"Well, I couldn't see her very well, with that veil and all," said Joan. "She is—rather a funny shape, isn't she?"

Maggie stared at her, outraged.

"Why, she has a most *lovely* figure! Her waist is only nineteen inches!"

"Oh!" said Joan, baffled more by the tone than by the words. "But ... she isn't really very slight, is she?"

"Well, of course not!" said Maggie, freshly outraged. "*Nobody* admires thin people!"

"Oh!" said Joan; and thought it well to give the subject a turn.

"Isn't it awfully difficult to see, through a veil with all those big spots?"

"Well, I suppose it is, rather: till you get used to it," said Maggie.

"And aren't they terribly hot?"

"I suppose they may be," Maggie owned. "But, of course, everyone has to wear a veil, if they want to look really smart. Mother says I shall have to wear one, on Sundays and so on, as soon as I put my hair up."

And Joan had been consistently thinking of Mrs. Corrie as thoroughly sensible and out of date, and without the least regard for fashion! She felt so stunned, that she let Maggie prattle on unheedingly, not troubling to listen.

"Look! There are Mildred and Eva again!" were the first words that came to her comprehension. And there they were—the lithe dark girl, and the big fair girl—standing by the sea-railing, talking hard.

"Why are they standing there? They don't seem to be looking at anything!"

"Oh, they're just arguing! They argue all the time—I don't think they agree about a single thing!"

"Then why do they go about together?"

"Why, they're the most *tremendous* chums!" said Maggie, astonished. "They hardly ever want anyone else."

"But what do they argue *about*?"

"Oh, history, mostly," said Maggie, in a casual manner. (And indeed, passing close but quite unobserved at that very moment, an indignant exclamation of "Charles James Fox, indeed!" came wafted on the sea-breeze.) "Mildred knows a lot, and she'll argue with *anybody*. I've heard her go on with Miss Knox—*Miss Knox*, who *teaches* history!—for ever so many minutes together, and stick to her own opinion at the end."

Joan cast a respectful backward glance at this daring heroine. History, as we already know, was not her own strong point.

"But of course," said Maggie, kind as usual, and anxious to be just, "it's just because she really does know a lot, and is really interested—not like Ella Tybald, who tries how far she

can go: she's *awful*. In French, the other day, she translated 'Un
mince filet de fumée s'éleva' as 'A smell of minced fillet rose
up,' and *stuck* to it that it was right. Mademoiselle was simply
furious! And she's worst of all in Latin; we're doing Virgil,
you know, and I don't think Miss Thwaites is very good at it
herself, and I think she's really frightened of Ella! You know
where Æneas calls his men 'O fessi graviora'?"

Joan mumbled a polite nothing.

"Well, Ella translated that 'O most indigestible raisin-
wine,' and Miss Thwaites *couldn't* make her own up that she
knew better. She said, quite gravely, that she had looked up
all the words, and *fessum* was raisin-wine, and if a thing was
heavy it must be indigestible. And another time she said that
Venus came to meet Æneas, 'bearing a bone'—'gerens os,' you
know—Oh, *look!*" exclaimed Maggie, "there *is* the Countess,
in this window!"

They had turned away from the sea-front, and were going
down a rather narrow dark street with shops on both sides;
and the photographer's, to which they had just come, had one
window quite full of pretty women. Not actresses; they didn't
look like that. Certainly not film-stars. Just the sort of portrait
that one sees in illustrated papers, of Lady Whatnot and her
Pet Peke, or The Duchess of Chose with Friend—only there
were no Pekingese or Alsatians, but pugs with funny bunched
faces, and enormous mastiffs or St. Bernards, and horrible
little skinny terriers that, one saw instinctively, must in real life
yap any house down.

"But who are all these people?" Joan inquired.

"Why, they're Society Beauties!" said Maggie, as if that
explained everything.

"But does anyone buy them?"

"Oh, I suppose so! ... See, this is the Creamery next door,
and Mother gave me some money for us to go there."

The Creamery was large and cool: not exactly a dairy, not

exactly a restaurant, though it had a certain likeness to both. You could buy there everything that you would naturally buy at a dairy: or you could sit in a comfortable chair before a little table, and enjoy fruit and cream, or ices, accompanied by simple things such as sponge-cakes or biscuits. There were a good many people there already, employed in this pleasant manner; but fortunately one table for two was left in a corner, and Maggie went over to it quickly.

"Well, what would you like?" she asked, with a beaming face.

"An ice-cream soda, please," said Joan, who was very hot.

"I'm sorry—a *what?*" asked Maggie doubtfully. And, on Joan's repeating her desire, she shook her head in a bewildered manner, and said she ... she was sorry, but she didn't know what that was, and she was afraid there wouldn't be any— whatever it was. Would Joan like an ice? She was very much distressed about it.

"What are *you* going to have?" Joan inquired.

"I'm going to have fruit and cream ... it's awfully good here."

"Then I will too, please," said Joan, anxious to oblige, and sorry to have upset the kind Maggie. And subsequently she was glad to have made this choice, for she had never tasted anything more delicious. The fruit was obviously fresh; the cream was obviously just rich thick cream and nothing else whatever. ... It struck Joan suddenly that that was exactly what she had been noticing, without knowing what it was, at every meal she had had in this strange old-new world. Everything was *real.* You couldn't imagine for a moment that there was any sort of make-shift, or that anything had been kept on ice or brought from overseas in a tin.

Taking her time over it, because it was so extremely nice, Joan looked about her; and noticed something unusual—she couldn't think what it was—about the people present. They were mostly young, and mostly well-dressed, according to the extraordinary standards of the time; that is, their clothes were all bunched and flounced and contorted, and stuck out to an incredible extent behind; and their waists were so small as to be unbelievable; and their front hair was curled, and their veils were tight and spotted. Joan discovered, watching, the mystery of this tightness, for a pretty girl opposite was just putting her veil down. She drew it as tight as it was possible to be, so that her very eyelashes were rumpled, and then twisted it cunningly under her chin and tucked in the end of the twist so that it didn't show. And Joan discovered also, all at once, what seemed queer and surprising—not one person there was in any way made up. They all wore their natural eyebrows as they had grown, and there didn't appear to be a lipstick in the place. She would have liked to ask Maggie about this; but it seemed a doubtful sort of question, and she prudently held her tongue.

One sight, however, surprised her so extremely that she *had* to ask. A thin, youngish woman came in—and that in itself was unusual, for these people of eighteen-ninety seemed to be naturally plump—and she was wearing over her mouth an extraordinary large black patch. Sitting down at a table, she removed this; and Joan saw that it was quite thick, and fastened round her ears with loops of black elastic.

"What is that ugly black thing?" she murmured cautiously to Maggie.

"That?" said Maggie, looking, and obviously not in the least surprised by what she saw. "Oh, that's only a respirator! I expect she's consumptive, poor thing."

"But what's it *for?*"

"Oh, to keep the air from her lungs, of course."

The air was, as has been said, sweet and warm, though there was a fresh little breeze. Joan stared with round eyes.

"But I thought consumptive people were sent to sanatoriums,

where they *lived* in fresh air: high up, in Switzerland: sleeping out in balconies, and never having their windows shut?"

"Sleeping out in the night air!" Maggie gasped, with the utmost horror. "Oh, *no!* Why, it would be the worst thing possible for them—bad for anyone, of course, but I should think it would *kill* anyone consumptive! And they are *never* sent to cold places like Switzerland; they go to Bournemouth, and Torquay, and Mentone, where the air is warm and soft. ... I am sure," with a return of her natural kind politeness, "you must be thinking of some other illness."

Joan knew perfectly well that she wasn't, having in mind a cousin of her mother's who had had a sleeping-porch specially built for him when he came back from his Swiss sanatorium; but she could be polite also.

"That respirator-thing must be very uncomfortable," she said mildly, looking at it as it lay on the table by its owner.

"Oh, horrid!" Maggie agreed at once. "She must be *really* ill; or you'd think just a cloud would be enough, on a fine day like this."

"A ... cloud?" Joan inquired politely.

"Oh, *you* know! Just a little fleecy woollen shawl, to wear round one's neck and over one's mouth, if one has a cold, or goes out on a very cold evening. *Everyone* wears them. ... Do you know, Effie has the most perfectly lovely fascinator, that an old nurse of ours made her for a wedding-present! Pale pink, with white bobbles all round her face. She looks *sweet* in it."

"I ... don't think I've ever seen one," Joan had to own.

"Oh, you *must* have! But perhaps," said the over-polite Maggie, "they are called something else where you live. A knitted hood, you know, to wear when people go out in the evening, to keep their hair tidy. ... But perhaps you haven't got a sister who is Out?"

Joan shook her head.

"That's it, of course, then," said Maggie. "Have you done? I think we'd better go, if you have, for so many people are coming in."

She paid, and they went out. As they passed the lady with the respirator, she was coughing horridly, a little nasty hacking cough, and her thin face had flushed, and her eyes looked unnaturally bright.

CHAPTER X

EIGHTEEN-NINETY TENNIS

THEY went back, not by the sea, but on the opposite side of the road where there were shops: very small shops they seemed to Joan, and containing very odd merchandise. The clothes-shops in particular fascinated her, until Maggie could hardly drag her away. Those incredible hats and bonnets and lace caps! Those strange, short, fussy coats and even fussier mantles: those unbelievably dowdy undergarments, plain and full and long-sleeved and thick with tucks: those wonderful "clouds" and "fascinators," of which Maggie had spoken as the natural wear of everyone! There was not a stocking that was not black, except a few frivolous brown ones draped over bronze shoes, or white ones that were connected only with white satin to dance in.

It was not only clothes, either. The fruit-shops struck her as wonderfully thin and poor, containing just ordinary vegetables and a very sparse selection of English fruits: cherries and gooseberries and currants and raspberries, with a few early cooking plums.

"Why are there no oranges or apples?" she inquired of Maggie: and was told: "Why, of course not! They're out of season now."

"How terribly dear the bananas are!" said Joan, with her eye on some small and wretched specimens labelled *3d.*

"Don't you think they're very nasty?" said Maggie.

"Why, no!" said Joan, in surprise. "I could eat dozens."

"Well, I've only tasted them once or twice," said Maggie. "Of course, it's only a little while since they began to come over. I suppose one could get *used* to them. Eva Dugan said that they had a great bunch sent, from cousins in Teneriffe, and nobody in the house liked them! But of course they *had* to eat them, and by the end of the bunch she thought they were rather nice."

Joan had moved on to the photographer's next door, and was attentively studying dresses and coiffures, which all struck her as singularly ugly.

"This is not a very good place, is it?" she said. "All the people look so terribly stiff!"

"It's much the best photographer's in Slonsea," said Maggie indignantly. "And how can they help being stiff? It's awfully hard to keep still for so long; and of course the clip that they put at the back of one's head *keeps* one in the same position— that's what it's for!"

"Oh!" said Joan blankly: remembering the careless way in which she had been told to sit, only last holidays, and the instantaneous click which had meant that it was all over. She was sorry to have given offence, without the slightest intention; but Maggie was her placid self again at once.

"I want to go in here and buy some sweets," she said.

Well, that at least had a pleasant and familiar sound! and Joan was pleased to find that she had a purse in her pocket, with several coins in it. She turned them out into her hand to see how much there was; and was struck by a curious coincidence.

"Why, how old they are!" she said. "They're all Queen Victoria …"

She broke off in a hurry; but fortunately Maggie, who was looking very blank, took it quite well when she had made an inspection.

"Yes, you haven't a single Jubilee one!" she said. "But I really think the old ones are prettier, when she was young and did her hair in a knot behind. … Do you know how to find the elephant on a florin?"

"No," said Joan truthfully; and was shown that rather disloyal coincidence; and they went into the shop, which was small and clean and pleasant, with a high counter on the right and sweets displayed on it in the usual way. But …

"How *awfully* cheap they are!" said Joan in a hurried whisper to Maggie, when the shop-girl had turned away to find something on a shelf.

"Oh, I don't think so," said Maggie, surprised. "This is rather a *good* shop. There *are* cheap ones, of course, and some of the sweets there are quite good, too. I know a very jolly one where caramels are twelve a penny."

"Twelve a *penny!*" said Joan.

"Yes. One of our girls found once that she had only a farthing in her pocket, and she was dared to go in and spend it; and she got her three all right—but the man wasn't awfully pleased."

Joan went on staring round her, open-eyed. All boiled sweets—bulls' eyes, and acid drops, and so on—seemed to be fourpence a pound; and the most expensive ones in the shop were never more than threepence-halfpenny a quarter. Ginger-beer and lemonade stood in rows at a penny a bottle; but spruce beer—whatever that might be—was three-halfpence. Maggie laid out one and threepence, and had as much as she could conveniently carry.

"Did you say you wanted to buy something?" she asked of Joan: who answered, bewildered, that she did, and was advised as to the best value for her money. Russian toffee was awfully good; and those pink and yellow things were jolly, too, if you didn't mind the little sprinkling of coconut on the top; and, if you liked peppermint, those big humbugs were two a penny, and scrumptious! Joan obediently followed these suggestions, and spent a shilling, and was glad that she hadn't loaded herself with more.

"It'll be hot playing tennis this afternoon," said Maggie,

as they came out into the glaring sunshine; and Joan agreed fervently. All her clothes seemed sticking to her, under her stiff stays; her feet, in the high black boots that seemed to attract the heat, were swollen and uncomfortable. She shifted her parcels into one hand and felt for her handkerchief, to rub her shiny face. ... These clothes were perfectly hateful, but they had one unexpected advantage; they had a large pocket in the skirt, easy to get at and holding anything one pleased. When she took out her purse, Joan had found herself, with surprise, possessed of a knife, a pencil, a piece of indiarubber, and a little spinning-top—it was almost as good as being a boy.

"Oh, wait a minute! I've got to get some biscuits for Mother," said Maggie; and turned into a grocer's. They were Osborne biscuits; and she produced a sixpence and a penny. "Mother always will have Osbornes, even though they are so expensive," she said confidentially to Joan.

"Expensive!" Joan gasped in reply; and, looking round, saw that ordinary kinds were fourpence or fivepence, or even less— and not any cheap and nasty makes, either; the familiar name and the familiar tin were just the same as ever. Joan looked also at other things and their prices; but they conveyed nothing to her. She had a general feeling that her mother would have had the shock of her life, if she had been present.

"What *is* that?" she asked Maggie, as they emerged again.

"That hansom, do you mean?" said Maggie, looking also at the queerest vehicle, standing waiting by the roadside. It was two-wheeled and high; and the driver sat perched up on a tiny seat behind, with his reins going over the roof and down in front to the horse, over which he seemed to have hardly any control at all.

"How on *earth* do you get in?" said Joan; but at that moment someone came out from the shop behind them and got in, showing her how in the most practical manner. He stepped up, threw back an odd sort of apron door that opened in halves,

sat down, and shut himself in again; there was only room for
two people, and Joan laughed to see him looking out over the
wooden apron, with the reins hanging down in front of his
face—it had the queerest effect.

"Don't you *like* them?" said Maggie, astonished. "Why,
they're lovely! They go so fast; it's almost like flying! I've been
in one with my uncle in London."

"Don't you ever go in them here, with your mother, if
they're so jolly?"

Maggie looked intensely shocked.

"Oh, *no!*" she said. "I don't think Mother would go in one at
all—and *certainly* not without a gentleman. You—you *couldn't.*"

"Why not?" Joan inquired blankly.

But Maggie didn't seem to know why not; she only knew,
without a shadow of doubt, that it couldn't be done, and
wasn't done, and ought not to be done.

Joan, annoyed, went back to a previous phrase.

"You said it was like flying—but it can't have been, you
know! Have you ever flown? I have!"

Maggie stared at her with the roundest eyes that Joan had
ever seen: which is saying much.

"*Flown?*" she said.

"Yes," said Joan, with her chin up. "From Croydon to Paris.
Mummy and I went last Easter. It was lovely!"

Maggie ceased to goggle, and burst into laughter that
sounded a good deal relieved.

"You did take me in!" she said. "I really thought you meant
it—I never knew you just meant a dream!"

Her relief was so simple and genuine, that Joan hadn't the
heart to argue out her point—besides, she saw quite well that
it wouldn't have been the least use. Maggie would only have
thought her a shameless liar or a lunatic—and either would
have been an unpleasant rôle to play, while staying as a guest
in the house. Joan looked instead, with interest, at the man in

the hansom arguing with his driver: who had opened a small
hole in the roof, and was talking down through it, in a red-
faced and loud-voiced manner. He appeared to get the better
of the argument in the end, and he flicked his horse smartly
and drove off—fast, certainly, but not in the least like flying, or
even a quick motor. Joan looked consideringly at Maggie. How
very, very odd it must be, not only never to have gone faster
than that—leaving trains, of course, out of the question—but
not to know that such a thing was possible! Yet Maggie seemed
perfectly contented: more contented and happy, in fact, when
one came to think it over, than any girl Joan had ever known.
Little things seemed to give her such entire pleasure. She didn't
seem to ask of life anything more than what fell naturally into
her hands.

She began quite suddenly, with no particular connection,
to tell Joan of Guy Fawkes' Day at Slonsea: of the enormous
towering guys that were dragged on trolleys along the sea-
front, men running beside with torches, little boys throwing
squibs, noise and laughter and excitement. "We lived on the
front when I was little," said Maggie, "and I used to *love* it."
The guys were burned, it seemed, in a bonfire somewhere
in the Old Town: much too rough a business for small girls.
And then the Circus! It also used to process along the parade,
with beautiful ladies in riding-habits on long-tailed horses, and
clowns, and elephants, and caravans with wild beasts inside,
and other caravans where the circus people lived, and clowns,
and Britannia sitting high up on the highest peak of all, with
her trident and her shield. It seemed to Joan that Maggie had
enjoyed the procession almost as much as the Circus itself,
which took place in a great tent set up in a field. And once
she had actually seen Grace—W. G.—playing cricket! And
that certainly gave Joan a shock, for it seemed going right
back into English history. ... But she was learning wisdom by
this time, and she did not mention Lord's, or Olympia, or the

Aldershot Tattoo. Maggie was perfectly happy with her simpler pleasures. It would have been useless—more: it would have been unkind—to try to make her understand the much more glorious amusements of the nineteen-thirties. And what would have been the use of mentioning Hobbs, for instance, when at this time he was a very small boy learning the rudiments of his game on Parker's Piece at Cambridge?

They had reached the house in the Square; and, O heavens, what a relief it was to be rid of that hat and those gloves! Joan came down from her room to hear Maggie's voice, rather high and lamentable.

"But, *Mother!* I was just going in to ask Ethel Truby and Dorothy Marrable!"

"I know, Maggie. I'm really sorry; but what was I to do, when they came and asked you, and I knew you had not made up a four with anyone else?"

"Yes," said Maggie mournfully. "I ... see. Oh, I know it wasn't *your* fault, Mother dear!"

"What's the matter?" Joan asked, coming in.

"Only I did want to have had two very jolly girls to play this afternoon—I couldn't ask them before you came, till I knew if you cared about it; and now the Derwents have asked us instead."

"Who are the Derwents?" Joan asked further.

Maggie answered that they lived next door, and they ... they didn't play very well. She wouldn't, or at any rate didn't, say more than that. But she was depressed, as Joan had never yet seen her, and very quiet all through luncheon: which, like all the other meals in this new world, was conspicuously good—and once more Joan was impressed with the *realness* of everything. That delicious leg of lamb had never travelled from New Zealand; those luscious stewed plums had not come out of any tin: no cream had ever, surely, been so rich and thick and satisfying.

"They're coming at three," said Maggie. "I think we'd better go early and secure a court—a lot of people play on Saturday afternoons."

They went across to the Square gardens, accordingly, as soon as luncheon was finished; and Joan observed, half-way across, that even for that tiny distance Maggie had put on her gloves and was glancing, a little unhappily, at her companion's bare hands—she even seemed relieved when they were once well inside the gate. One or two courts were already occupied; so they went on to those nearest the sea-front, which were a little worn. Joan paused for a minute to look at one which struck her as unusual.

"Oh, we don't want to play on a hard court to-day!" said Maggie, misunderstanding. "In hot weather the asphalt *does* melt so; and then it sticks to one's shoes."

"The what?" asked Joan.

"The asphalt," said Maggie.

It was a greyish-black court, with a surface not unlike a newly-tarred road; and here and there, without anyone on it, there were already melting patches which glistened in the sun. Joan was very glad indeed that they were not going to play there. Maggie chose one of the further grass-courts, and put down her racket and balls in the middle of it to show that it was taken; then she called upon Joan to help her pull up the net, which was at present sagging in the most dismal manner.

"But there's no winder!" said Joan, going helpfully up to the post.

"No *what?*" asked Maggie, in her turn.

"No winder. How do you pull it up?"

"Why, by the ropes, of course!" said Maggie, staring.

They were guy-lines like those of a tent, fastened into the grass with pegs, two at each end of the net, splaying out on to the grass outside the court. It was not a very easy or a very pleasant job, in that hot sun. If you pulled too hard, the pegs came out with a plop; if you didn't pull hard enough, the net remained with a discouraged droop in the middle. By the time that it was pulled up to something like tautness—there was no wire rope through it, only a thin cord—both girls were very glad to sit down and cool off: as far as that was possible in a perfectly shadeless garden.

"You've got a new racket," said Joan politely. "How jolly!"

Maggie handed it over for examination, with pride and pleasure; and Joan felt a sort of homesick joy to see a familiar name on the familiar fish-tail handle.

"Yes, it's quite new," said Maggie. "It takes such ages to save up!"

"Doesn't it!" Joan agreed; and privately wondered what Maggie's pocket-money might be. She herself had only managed to get a new racket last year with various outside aids, including the fortunate fact that her birthday fell in April.

"Thirteen-and-nine *is* a lot of money for just a racket," said Maggie, with a sigh.

"I ... *how* much did you say?"

"Thirteen-and-nine," said Maggie again; and showed, for confirmation, the price stamped on the handle. It seemed to Joan (who had paid more than three times that) little short of a miracle.

"Did you get it in a Sale?"

"In a what?"

"In a Sale—a London Sale."

"You don't mean a Sale of Work?"

"Oh, *no!*"

"I just bought it in a shop," said Maggie, in her usual state of slight bewilderment.

"Then ... are they *always* that price?" Joan gasped.

"Yes, of course!" said Maggie, staring at her. "I showed you—it's stamped on the handle. ... Oh, there they are!"

She jumped up, and went to meet two girls who had just come in at the nearest gate; and Joan followed, looking at them with a little curiosity. She wanted to see why Maggie had been so reluctant to play with them.

One was tall, and one—obviously the elder—was short; and the first thing that struck Joan was their amazing waists—she really believed that she could have spanned that of the short one with her two hands. The other girl, who was on a much bigger scale, had a figure exactly like that of an hourglass: which, though tolerable in a wasp, struck Joan as quite hideous in a girl. She was a red girl—hair, and cheeks, and, unfortunately, nose as well, and she walked stiffly and awkwardly—but that they both did. The shorter elder girl would have been very pretty indeed if she had had a better complexion; as it was, even in that hot sun, she was very much the colour of an old candle. She had a gushing manner and an affected voice; but she was exceedingly pleasant to Joan, and professed herself delighted to come and play. Her sister seemed a silent person, who grinned agreeably but had no conversation.

"Well, let's play!" said Maggie; and then, of course, followed the usual embarrassing discussion as to *how* they should play, with compliments to Maggie from her two schoolfellows— evidently she was considered something of a pro. The tall Cicely got out, gruffly, that she herself was "no good." The short Mabel cried gushingly that *she* was a perfect *silly*. Joan, who knew herself to be a strictly moderate performer, was suitably modest. Finally they tossed for it, and she and Mabel drew together.

"I *am* sorry for you," said her partner coquettishly.

"Well, I'm pretty mouldy," said Joan: which seemed, for some unknown reason, to surprise her companion very much. She stared at Joan with her large and pretty eyes, and had nothing whatever to say for the moment. ... It struck Joan as odd, considering the sort of girls they seemed to be, and the fact that Mabel looked at least seventeen, that neither of them was in the least made up—not even a powdered nose.

What a relief it was, after those unspeakable boots, to be wearing shapeless, hideous sand-shoes! which seemed the correct tennis-wear for everyone, large and small. How joyfully Joan tossed off her detestable hat, and threw it on the seat where she had been sitting. ...

"You aren't going to play without a *hat!*" Mabel cried, in quite a natural and unaffected voice of horror.

"Why, of course!" said Joan. "I always do."

"But not in hot sun like this, surely?" said Maggie hurriedly.

"Yes. *Always*," said Joan, in a firm voice. (She really had to draw the line somewhere; and this was, quite evidently, the place to do it.)

"But not in a public place like the Gardens?" Mabel urged.

"*Anywhere*," said Joan, more firmly still.

"But it will look so queer!" the comparatively speechless Cicely got out, with agitation.

Joan didn't answer that at all. She left her hat where it was, and marched with a determined step on to the court. ... What! Play with that hateful, stiff sailor-hat perched on the top of her head, straining at its elastic leash with every movement? Not much! And what idiotic nonsense, to make such a fuss about it! If she had been proposing to play without stockings, now, as so many people do nowadays. ...

It wasn't nowadays. It was thenadays: a very different proposition. But, for all that, Joan *would not wear that hat.*

"How are we going to play?" she asked Mabel: who answered faintly: "Oh! *You* serve!" as if she hadn't got over the shock yet.

Though she was a good deal rattled by all this controversy, Joan made no bones about it, but served hard: into the net: twice.

"*Sorry!*" she said, much annoyed with herself. (After all, it wasn't an unpardonable crime. Why should Mabel be again looking at her like that?)

"Do you always serve like that?" she inquired, in a strained voice.

"Into the net?" said Joan: flushed, and thinking it a very rude comment. "No. Not quite always!"

"No, *no!* Of course I didn't mean that. But—like a man."

"I wish I *did* serve like a man!" said Joan ruefully.

"But you *do*," Mabel persisted.

The argument seemed likely to lead nowhere; and Joan hated talking while she played. She served again, successfully, to Cicely, who gave a slight scream and dodged: to Maggie, who made a valiant swipe and missed it: to Cicely again, with exactly the same result as before: to Maggie, who hit back into the net. Game.

By the time they reached Four Love, Joan saw what it was all about. Everyone but herself served under-hand: Maggie placed her balls well enough, but quite mildly: the two Derwents lobbed theirs up to a surprising height, and sometimes these fell on the right side of the net and sometimes they didn't. ... It was, in fact, as Miss Pugh her Games Mistress would have said with no uncertain voice, merely pat-ball.

"I say!" said Mabel gaspingly, when that love-sett came to an end. "I'm glad I wasn't playing against you!"

"Do all the girls at your school play as hard as you?" Maggie inquired, with honest admiration.

"Oh, *I'm* no good!" said Joan modestly. "You should see Jane Harvey—she's our Games-Captain."

"Your *what?*" Maggie and Cicely inquired together. Mabel seemed too much out of breath to say another word.

"Our Games-Captain."

There was another of those brief, uncomfortable silences, to which Joan was by this time becoming quite accustomed. Then Maggie inquired how they should play now.

"Oh, let's have a long rest first!" Mabel panted out; and she dropped on to the nearest seat, like the worn-out fetter in the poem—and yet she certainly hadn't exerted herself much! She had never run at all: merely moved stiffly to meet a coming ball, or served even more stiffly when her turn came—creaking, as Joan was forced to observe, every time she moved. But she looked absolutely exhausted: not flushed, but even a sallower tallow-colour than before. Her sister was like a beetroot; and Maggie's brow was wet with honest sweat, as if she had been playing for hours. ... It was, of course, their dreadful clothes. Joan could sympathise there, for, after even an extremely mild sett like this, she was more uncomfortably hot than she had ever been in her life before: everything was sticking to her, and her stays prevented her from refreshing herself with a good deep breath. A daring suggestion occurred to her: quite unjustified by any of the other players in the Gardens, as she cast hopeful glances in all directions. Still, she would chance it!

"Wouldn't it be much cooler if we played the next sett without stockings?" she said.

"Without *what?*" the silent Cicely almost screamed.

"*Stockings*," said Joan, in a voice which sounded, even to herself, unnaturally loud and brazen. She found herself looking from one to another of them in a defiant manner. It was so *stupid* of them to be looking so unutterably shocked! They couldn't have seemed more so if she had suggested playing without any clothes at all.

"Well ... nobody does, you see," said Maggie at last, trying as usual to be kind and tactful.

"They *do!*" Joan persisted hotly. "I've *seen* them ... at Wimbledon, and lots of places besides!"

"Perhaps you've played like that yourself?" Mabel suggested, with a silly giggle, and a glance, meant to be arch, at the other two.

"Well, of course I have!" said Joan.

A silence of horror fell around her—she could feel it quite distinctly. Mabel stopped giggling, and looked positively alarmed. Cicely simply stared Maggie, turning a lively purple, rose decidedly from the seat.

"I'm afraid it wouldn't do here," she said. "Shall we play another sett?"

CHAPTER XI

The Gordian Knot

THEY played one more sett, with precisely similar results, though the two Derwents had changed partners: a love-sett for Joan and Cicely. Then, after another rest, they went in to tea. Mrs. Corrie was quite distressed by the hotness of all of them, and said that they really ought not to have played at all so early, considering the heat of the day; but it never occurred to her, obviously, that clothes might be blamed as well as temperature. She thought that they had better wash—which all were glad enough to do—and then keep quite quiet for the twenty minutes before tea would be ready. She then went into the drawing-room, and shut the door; and the four girls, to Joan's surprise, went into the dark dining-room as a matter of course, and stayed there by themselves.

As Mabel cooled down, her power of chat seemed to return. She prattled of this and that—school-affairs—to Maggie; and then turned, in a freshly affected manner, and inquired if Joan had had many valentines this year.

"Many *what?*" (It really seemed to Joan that she had never heard or used that short, impolite interrogation so many times in her life, as during the last few hours.)

"Valentines! *I* never had so many!" said Mabel, with a little gratified simper. And Cicely chimed in: and even the sensible Maggie owned, with satisfaction, to having had four, and never having found out who was the sender of one of these. Joan knew, of course, what was meant: one met Valentines in old numbers of *Punch*, and in "What Katy Did." But she really was surprised at Maggie. ...

"*Wasn't* it a lark about Dora Timson!" Mabel exclaimed finally, with much laughter.

"*Rather!*" Cicely chimed in.

"Yes. But it was rather a shame," said Maggie, a little awkwardly.

"What happened?" inquired Joan, tired of being outside the conversation—though they had never meant to make her feel like that; they simply couldn't imagine the possibility of a world that didn't send Valentines.

"Well, she's in the Sixth," said Maggie, rather slowly. "And ..."

"Not a bit pretty!" said Mabel, with a satisfied glance into the glass opposite.

"A face like chalk," said the rubicund Cicely.

"And rather bossy, and nobody likes her awfully," Maggie went on in a hurry, as if she thought enough had been said. "Anyhow, it must be rather horrid to be as old as that and ... and probably not get any Valentines at all. And this year she got one—addressed to her at school—and she was rather pleased about it, and let people know, and hadn't the least idea who sent it."

"And when she opened it," Mabel took up the tale with gusto, "a little packet of rouge fell out, and a poem, printed in big letters, so that people couldn't help seeing what it said!" She stopped to giggle. "I can't remember exactly—it was awfully clever, and just like her. ..."

"It was awfully rude," said Maggie uncomfortably. But she wouldn't say, when asked, if she remembered the words of the unflattering poem.

"She made an awful fuss," Mabel went on, with relish. "She very nearly *cried*; and then Miss Knox came in, and asked what was the matter—and Dora *told* her!"

"What happened then?" Joan inquired, rather taken aback. It really did seem an extraordinarily babyish thing to be taken up by any mistress; but these girls of the 'nineties apparently expected to have everything arranged for them.

"Oh, Miss Knox knows most things! She knew at once who had sent it—so did we all, of course. It was Ella Tybald—she *is* awful. But she said she never had, and stuck to it; and then Miss Knox caught Gertie Lewis grinning, and remembered how awfully good she is at printing things, and saw through the whole thing at once. Ella had really *done* it all, of course— she's awful! But she'd got Gertie to do the printing and post the envelope, so that she could say she'd never sent it—she knew she'd be asked, of course. There *was* a row."

It seemed to Joan—when she had disentangled the various "she's" mentioned in this sorry tale—that it was a piffling sort of business, and that a Sixth Form girl of these times must be pretty feeble. But Maggie and Mabel and Cicely so evidently considered the whole thing an event, that it might be rude of a mere visitor if she appeared to think little of it; and, of course, there was an easy side-way out.

"Well," said Joan conversationally, "I suppose this Dora is just leaving school, if she's in the Sixth now? So she'll soon be able to use make-up as much as she likes!"

There was a shocked and terrible silence: broken at last by Maggie, making haste to change the subject once for all. She looked quite pale, in spite of the heat, and she glanced uneasily at the door—which was, fortunately, tight shut.

"How *did* you learn to play tennis so well?" she asked of Joan.

"Well, I don't," said Joan honestly. "But I'm terribly fond of it, of course; and Miss Pugh, our Games Mistress, is an awfully good coach."

There was the usual rather blank pause: succeeded by the usual word.

"Your *what?*"

"Our Games Mistress."

"But *what* did you say she was?"

"I said she was a jolly good coach; and so she is," said Joan warmly. She wasn't going to retract that perfectly harmless phrase, even if it did sound slangy to these extraordinarily unsophisticated ears.

"But—what *is* a Games Mistress?" Maggie inquired slowly. "You can't mean a mistress who teaches *games?*"

"Why not?" asked Joan blankly. "Haven't you got one at your school? Oh, bad luck! But who teaches gym., and dancing, and all that sort of thing?"

"Oh!" said Maggie. "Madame Balbo comes down from London once a week, to teach dancing and Deportment—I didn't know you meant *that.*"

"What's Deportment?" Joan inquired in her turn, blankly.

"Why, how to walk well, and to curtsey, and to introduce people—all that sort of thing!"

Joan stared as much as politeness allowed. Why *should* one have lessons in introducing people? One learnt all that by the light of nature, noticing the way one's mother did it at parties and Lord's, and so on.

"But she doesn't teach games?"

"Madame Balbo? Oh, *no!*"

The two Derwents broke into irrepressible and violent giggling; and even Maggie allowed herself to smile broadly—though she apologised for it at once.

"You've never seen her, of course, Joan. One simply can't imagine Madame without her long black satin gown, and her little handkerchief in her hand, and her mittens!"

"*Mittens?*" Joan murmured faintly; and a frenzied vision came to her of St. Aldate's Miss Pugh, in the briefest possible drill-slip, teaching that very jolly dance, the sailor's hornpipe.

"But why," Cicely wanted to know, "should anyone *teach* games? One just *plays;* you can't learn it like a lesson!"

Another vision came to Joan, of being bowled to at the

nets by Miss Pugh on a hot July evening—just as serious a matter, in its own way, as any other lesson, and even more humiliating if one played wrong. But it was, of course, quite impossible to explain all this—and it was only too evident that none of these girls had been given any tennis-lessons at all. They had just picked it up haphazard; as Cicely had truly said, they "just played."

"What else do you play, besides tennis?" seemed a harmless question. Besides, Joan was really a little curious to know.

"Oh, cricket—up to the Fifth."

"Why not after that?"

"Well, how *could* one play in a long skirt?" said Cicely reasonably. Joan saw the reasonableness of it at once.

"What else? What do you play in the winter?"

"Oh, nothing in the *winter*, of course!" they all answered together, with obvious astonishment. "What is there to play?"

"Why, hockey or lax, of course!"

There was one of the usual, blank pauses. Then Maggie said that she had once seen boys playing hockey; and—what *was* lax?

"Lacrosse," Joan explained, biting off her reply rather short without saying "of course." She had said it so very often, that it began to sound rather rude. None of them had ever heard of the game, by either of its two names; which was at once damping and exasperating.

"Well, what *do* you do in the winter?" she cried.

"Why, of course one can go to the Baths, until it gets too cold; and even then it's all right, if one wears a cloud walking home," said Maggie. "And there's always riding, for the people who ride. And of course one goes for walks."

"Oh!" said Joan, of the generation that has almost forgotten how to walk. "Is that ... all?"

"Well, walking is always jolly—except when it's very hot, like to-day," said Maggie, of the generation that had to walk or stay indoors. She was quite indignant about it. "There are most awfully jolly walks all round Slonsea!" she said. "The Old Town; and up on the cliffs: and behind the town the country is *lovely!*"

The topic was evidently too incompatible; and Joan, seeing even placid Maggie a little ruffled, jumped hastily from the frying-pan into the fire by inquiring, without stopping to think, if they were Guides. (She knew, of course, the moment the words had left her lips, that the Derwents at least couldn't possibly be, with those waists and that affected giggling.)

"What *are* Guides?" Maggie inevitably inquired, quite polite and pleasant again.

Joan gave it up. She *couldn't* explain—and what would be the use? She could only answer vaguely: "Oh, a sort of … of Club!" and then sit silent, facing a world in which there were no winter games, no Guides, no Scouts, no … no anything, in fact. It had a truly terrible aspect for her—and yet Maggie seemed so happy and contented! She really was a marvel; for this present life, to eyes accustomed to the nineteen-thirties, looked *grim*—there was no other word for it.

Tea came in, perhaps fortunately, at this juncture—the table had, of course, been well and truly laid, all this time, with all manner of good things, and equally of course the guests had politely ignored it. The large bell outside rang loudly. Mrs. Corrie came in from the drawing-room. They all sat down round the table.

There had been plenty of time to cool down, and Joan was by this time very hungry: an excellent thing to be, in the face of such a spread. There was brown and white bread, and home-made jam, and shrimps, and three kinds of cake, and gooseberries and cherries; but Maggie began to lament, almost at once, that she had forgotten to tell her mother that Joan liked bananas—she *was* sorry.

"You don't *really*, do you?" said Mabel, with a little affected shriek of surprise. "Oh, I think they're *horrid*—I really do!"

Whatever her feelings for bananas, Joan was by this time pretty sure that she didn't like either of the Derwents. Her voice was a little stiff as she asked, in return, if Mabel liked grape-fruit; and was answered, more affectedly than ever: "Oh, yes, I *adore* grapes—especially black ones!" Cicely, on the other side, gave a little giggle; and Joan's tone was more than stiff as she answered:

"I didn't say grapes. I said *grape-fruit*."

"Is that something different?" Maggie inquired peaceably.

"Of course," said Joan.

"I'm afraid we haven't had it, down here," said Mrs. Corrie. "Mabel, my dear, you are eating nothing."

"Oh, yes, *indeed*, Mrs. Corrie!" said Mabel; and chose the smallest biscuit on a plate, and nibbled at it in a half-hearted manner. It occurred to Joan that perhaps, with a waist like that, you couldn't eat very much; there seemed no place to put it! It might be possible, of course, that Mabel was slimming, which would be comprehensible; but then, in this strange world people seemed to admire plumpness—so that couldn't be the explanation. Cicely, at any rate, was eating in a solid and silent manner, and getting redder and redder as she ate. It really was very unfortunate for a girl of her age—or of any age, for that matter—to have a nose like a beetroot.

"Are you going to hear Grossmith next week?" Maggie asked of Mabel: who said, in a faint and uninterested voice, that she didn't know—she supposed so.

"Don't you think he's *splendid?*" Maggie pursued enthusiastically. "We are so sorry it wasn't this Saturday, so that we could have taken Joan."

"What is he?" Joan inquired, gratified but ignorant.

"Haven't you ever heard him? Oh, he gives the most splendid entertainment—just himself with a piano, and nobody to help at all. One laughs all the time!"

"Is he at the theatre?" Joan inquired further. She had seen the local theatre, when she was out with Maggie in the morning. But, surprisingly, Maggie seemed to consider the inquiry rather odd and almost shocking. Oh, *no!* He appeared at the Concert Hall. It was quite evident that she had never been to the theatre in her life; and Joan, who knew vaguely that there were people who didn't approve of acting, considered it polite to change the subject—and, a minute later, was astounded to hear Mrs. Corrie mentioning that Effie had so very much liked a play that she saw last week. ... Apparently this was one more of the inexplicable things that were suitable for people who were Out, but not for schoolgirls. Or perhaps it was only suitable for people who were married!

At this point Mabel gave a queer little gasp: slowly toppled over from her chair, and fell in a crumpled heap between it and Joan's, which was next. Her face was as nearly green as it is possible for a human face to be. Everybody jumped up in consternation; and Mrs. Corrie hastily drew her out from among the chair and table legs, so that she could lie flat.

"She's only fainted," said Cicely, in a thick voice; and Joan saw, to her surprise, that neither she nor Maggie seemed very much surprised.

"She has done this before, then?" said Mrs. Corrie, in rather an odd dry voice.

"Oh, yes!" said Cicely, as a matter of course. "Often at home; and twice in school."

Mrs. Corrie was hastily unfastening the many buttons of Mabel's frock, and then the several buttons of her incredibly tight cotton under-bodice. She tried to put a finger under her stays; and couldn't do it. She tried to unfasten the stays; and couldn't do that either. Her face was a little stern and grim. Turning Mabel sideways, she attacked the stay-lace behind; but it was pulled absolutely taut, and the knot was quite hard.

"Scissors, please, Maggie."

But scissors, when Maggie had fetched them, were of no use either; it was impossible to get even the tip of the small blade under the lace. Mrs. Corrie, looking very stern indeed, got up and took the sharp bread-knife; and that, at last, did the job. There was a snap like the breaking of elastic. The lace, near where it was cut, ran rapidly through several holes; and Mrs. Corrie's fingers quickly managed the rest. The stays gaped several inches apart, where they had been pulled absolutely tight; and Mabel gave a sort of gasp, and opened her eyes. A blotchy colour came into her face, for the first time since Joan had met her, as she realised what was happening.

"Mrs. Corrie, I'm *so* sorry to have been so silly!" she said, still rather faintly; and she sat up on the floor.

"Yes, my dear," said Mrs. Corrie. "I think you have been very silly—if you like to call it by so mild a name—for a long time. Maggie shall lend you her golf-cape to go home in; for of course you will not be able to fasten your dress."

So, in an extraordinary shapeless garment that buttoned loosely down the front, Mabel retired to her home next door: neither she nor Cicely finding anything to say for themselves except vaguely murmured good-byes.

"How can she *stand* it!" Joan exclaimed, when they were gone.

"She has stood it for so long, that she is probably used to it now," said Mrs. Corrie. "But how she ever drew the laces so tight ..."

"Oh, I know that!" Maggie supplied, rather shame-facedly. "Cicely told me. They lace each other up, with the bed-post for a pulley. Of course I couldn't *say* much, because their mother ... Well, Cicely told me, too, that she goes to *bed* in her stays!"

"How awful!" Joan exclaimed.

"Much more awful than either of you can understand," said

Mrs. Corrie incisively. "Of course it is necessary for everyone to have some sort of support; but there is no possible excuse for tight-lacing."

Joan stared at her. Why should everyone need supporting? What were their backbones *for?* She herself had never known the meaning of weariness and backache till she put on the stays which she was wearing now. They weren't tight, of course; in fact, they were as loose as she could make them. But she was conscious of them all the time, and she knew very well that she was not breathing as she used to breathe, or feeling comfortable as she used to feel.

CHAPTER XII

CRASH!

THERE was still, of course, a long time before supper; and this evening (Joan being now attired according to Mrs. Corrie's ideas of propriety) they went out and sat on the beach, under a groyne that sheltered them from the hot westering sun. Both girls were rather subdued: Maggie on account of the Derwents, Joan because she was thinking of very different matters. She had now had a solid twenty-four hours—rather more—of eighteen-ninety life; and her old world seemed incredibly remote, desirable, and out of reach. It wasn't, of course, only clothes and that sort of thing; she was more or less uncomfortable, all the time—but it wasn't that. Few of us have ever experienced the painfulness of realising that our friends are not yet born, and that our mother is a baby of less than a year old. There was a lump in Joan's throat. She did not feel at all inclined to talk.

Maggie broke the rather chastened silence by asking: "Do you like Dickens?" (Books are, of course, a safe subject, warranted to hurt nobody's feelings.) It surprised Joan very much to find not only that Maggie had read a great deal, but that she seemed to remember nearly all of it: though there was, astonishingly, no school library. All house-books that she was allowed to read (Mrs. Corrie was evidently extremely strict) had been read over and over again; others she had borrowed from friends. She must spend positive hours a day reading. ...

"But how do you find the *time?*"

"Why, there's plenty of time!" said Maggie, looking surprised. "Not so much in the summer, of course, because of tennis and cricket; but the long winter evenings are splendid for getting through books."

Of course, when Joan came to think of it, they must be. If you cut out all winter games, and substitute a mere tame daily walk: if you have no Guides, and there is no motoring for anyone: if you are not allowed to go to the theatre, and there are no cinemas—why, you *must* read in self-defence. Another strange fact leaked out very soon; Maggie was never, under any consideration, allowed out after dark by herself, or even with another girl—she was plainly horrified at the mere idea, and she spoke with bated breath of Mildred Ayres, who had been brought up a good deal abroad and was generally recognised to be unconventional, as having been seen out alone, on a winter evening, *as late as eight o'clock.*

"Why not?" Joan inquired, considerably staggered. But the question shocked Maggie even more—though she seemed to have the vaguest ideas of what unknown harm would befall the daring girl who walked alone after sunset. Of course Effie came round sometimes to see her mother in the evening, when her husband was out; but then *she* was married.

"What difference does that make?" Joan inquired further, even more astonished; and Maggie didn't know, any more than she had known the answer to the previous question. It just was so. Married people were protected in some miraculous way from the dangers of the dark—perhaps, Joan reflected madly, it might be the wearing of bonnets! People who weren't married had, of course, to stay in after dark, unless they were suitably chaperoned. ... Why, the old Misses Homes, next door—and the youngest of them must be at least sixty!— never dreamed even of going out to tea in the winter unless their housemaid came to see them home. ... Was she very old and grim? Oh, *no*! Quite young, and rather pretty: about the same age as Sarah.

The whole thing seemed to Joan completely mad; but

Maggie evidently took it all as just a matter of course—as much a matter of course as the fact that no girl might ever read any newspaper. She had no reason for this, either: it was simply a taboo—"not nice for girls." When you had said that, apparently, you had said everything that there was to say, and the matter was at an end.

"Do you read the whole of every evening, all the winter?" Joan inquired, rather dismally. The idea seemed appalling: though she herself liked reading well enough, in a general way.

But Maggie said No, they played games: backgammon, and draughts—and Mother was awfully good at chess, but Maggie herself couldn't manage that at all. When girls came to tea, they played paper games: Telegrams, Consequences, that sort of thing. Bridge? What was *Bridge?* Maggie not only knew nothing about it, but she seemed pretty sure that it had never been heard of by anyone. There was whist, of course; but she herself was stupid at card games, and never could remember the different leads.

"But how can you go out to tea, if you mayn't go out alone after dark?" Joan inquired; and was instructed that the practically invariable plan was to go for a walk in the afternoon, return to tea, and be "fetched" at about seven, usually by Sarah. It made no difference whether the distance was great or small. Maggie could not possibly return alone even from her particular chum's, Ethel Truby, who lived two minutes away at the top of the Square, on the same side of the road; and Ethel Truby, in the same way, was "fetched" when she came to tea with Maggie. Only the unconventional Mildred Ayres was allowed to come and go independently; and even she was not considered sufficient escort for her special chum Eva Dugan, when it was Eva's turn to go to tea with her. She had offered, it appeared, again and again, to walk back with her; but no. Mrs. Dugan's housemaid (not quite seventeen: only a couple of months, in fact, older than Mildred) must "fetch" in the approved manner.

It was rather a boring subject, anyway. Joan's eyes, wandering up to the Parade, remained there, widening.

"That bath-chair looks terribly unsafe!" she said. "It's far too near the edge."

"They always talk of putting a railing all along, instead of just near the band-stand," said Maggie, looking too. "But it never gets done. That's Elsie Maxwell's mother in the chair, and Elsie with her. I wish she'd come down here. It's so awfully dull for her, getting no tennis all this summer."

"Why not? Has she been ill?" Joan inquired, looking up at a smallish girl in black, standing beside the chair and gazing rather wistfully at some late bathers.

"Oh, no! But her father died in the spring; and of course she is not doing any amusing things yet," said Maggie, waving to the wistful figure.

"Why not?" Joan inquired, mystified.

"Well, of course not, while she's in such deep mourning!" said Maggie, in a really shocked voice. "Oh, she's coming! That's all right."

The smallish figure had walked demurely down steps on to the beach: had stopped to wave: had started to run, like any ordinary girl: had recollected itself, and come on slowly and decorously. As it came near enough to be seen distinctly, Joan thought that she had never seen any person wearing such heavy mourning. On that hot summer evening, and though she could not have been more than fourteen at the outside, she wore a dull black frock of some woollen stuff—thin, but distinctly woollen—trimmed with crape nearly to the knees; and her black straw hat was also trimmed with a heavy twist of crape. Being small and fair, all this was particularly conspicuous. She was, of course, wearing black shoes and stockings, and black gloves; and she did not take these last off, as Maggie and Joan had gladly done, the moment they set foot on the beach. She chose carefully a dry place on the pebbles, and took pains to pull her skirt into place as she sat down.

"It's dreadful how crape spots and creases!" she said, with a sigh.

"Yes, isn't it!" Maggie agreed, in a heartfelt manner—it was quite evident that she had similar vivid and disagreeable memories. "I'm so sorry that you'll have to wear it all through the hot weather."

Elsie sighed again; and the kind Maggie quickly began to talk of school interests, which, it appeared, even people in mourning were allowed to share—but even this was difficult, and full of pitfalls. Lessons were, of course, quite safe, and so were tales of Ella Tybald the Awful: though Elsie pulled herself up once or twice, and glanced guiltily towards her mother in the bath-chair, as if laughter of any sort was not quite compatible with crape. But a school expedition to London (the Royal Academy and the British Museum) had been considered unduly frivolous; and of course the School Dance, which the Headmistress gave at the end of the summer term, would be entirely out of the question. Joan gathered, listening with astonishment and horror, that the heavy crape-trimmed dresses would be worn for six months, during which no sort of festivity could be allowed; and that for another six months dead black (without crape) would be necessary, but perhaps an occasional not too jovial amusement, such as a concert, might be conceded. Parties in general, and dances in particular, would be taboo for the entire twelve months. ... Joan felt that it all really must be quite unbearable! Bad enough, in all conscience, to lose one's father—a lump came into her throat at the bare thought—but how much worse to have the loss rubbed into one at every turn, like this. ... She suddenly found an awful sort of chuckle forcing its way through the choking lump, and had extreme difficulty in suppressing it. It was quite impossible that *she* should ever be called upon to go through this dreadful experience—for her mother was still only a year old, and her father must be about the age of a small boy playing near, wearing a sailor suit with long trousers and (incredibly) long yellow curls like a girl's, under his sailor hat, and reaching to his shoulders.

It was quite a relief when Elsie and Maggie caught sight of an Old Girl whom they knew, instantly becoming very much excited, and anxious to show her to Joan.

"Up there, near Mother's bath-chair! ... That's her fiancé with her. ... Do you know," in a hushed and impressive voice, "she was engaged in the holidays, directly after she left school, and she was only just eighteen! She'll be *married* before she's nineteen."

"Like Effie!" Maggie hastily put in, anxious lest her own heroine's glory should be diminished.

From the tones of both, Joan perceived that the Old Girl in question (who seemed, in the distance, to possess the smallest waist and fluffiest fringe that she had yet seen) had distinguished herself indeed. If she had taken her Double First at Oxford, or had flown from Australia to England, she couldn't have created a deeper impression—and, in the eyes of the nineteen-thirties, this was piffle. Joan had been quite meek and absorbent for some time. She now turned restive.

"*He* doesn't look anything very much," she said. "What a little thing he is! and what queer clothes!"

Maggie, reproachfully, said that he couldn't help either of these things—not his height, naturally; and she believed he was very poor. No, she didn't know exactly what he did; no, she owned that he wasn't handsome; no, she had never heard that he was at all clever. But what did all these things matter, compared with the magnificent fact that Doris would be married before she was nineteen—able to wear a bonnet, able to go out by herself after dark, able to do all those daring and delightful things that were forbidden to much older spinsters!

Joan, still restive, put her nose in the air. She didn't see why the prospect was so very wonderful—she wasn't at all sure that, for her own part, she wouldn't rather go out and earn her own living!

The two Victorian girls sat staring at her, speechless: until at last Maggie, with a gasp, said faintly:

"You wouldn't *like* to do that, without being *obliged?*"

"I shouldn't mind a bit!" Joan declared, still on her high horse.

"You wouldn't *like* to be a governess?" said Elsie, in a hushed voice.

"No, rather not!" said Joan. "But I shouldn't do that."

"Oh! You mean you'd like to be a hospital nurse?" said Maggie.

"No," said Joan. "I should hate it."

The two other girls spoke in concert, very solemnly. They said:

"But there *isn't* anything else!"

Joan forgot her century, and answered hastily.

"What nonsense! There are heaps of other things! I'd rather like to be a doctor, if it wasn't such a fearfully long training: and I'd really love to be a vet., only that's even longer—but I do love beasts, particularly horses. I've known ever so many girls who trained in Domestic Science, and got topping jobs, with quite big screws; and then there's Infant Welfare, of course, and Froebel—but they're no good unless you really like kids and get on well with them, and of course teaching is no good unless you go to Oxford or Cambridge, because you must have a degree to get anything worth having. Our last School Captain is training to be a Lady Almoner, and she loves it. Of course you have to be terribly good at games, if you take up Physical Culture and go in for being a Games Mistress. ..."

The phrase brought her back, sharply, to a sense of where she was, and what had been said on that subject before; and she broke off short. Maggie and Elsie were both staring at her with real concern, as if they believed her to be out of her mind—as they probably did. They had drawn a little away from her. They were bewildered and quite speechless. When Maggie did manage to answer, it was in a voice that was studiously gentle and soothing and considerate.

"Yes," she said. "Oh, yes, of course! You ... you must be, I'm sure."

Elsie, younger and less tactful, was still staring hard.

"What a queer school yours must be!" she said bluntly.

"It's a terribly good school!" said Joan, up in arms at once for St. Aldate's. "We had a higher percentage of credits in the Certificate, last year, than any other school in England! And we won *all* our lax matches, and our tennis Six has only been beaten once this summer, so far. ..."

"Yes, I'm *sure* it's a very good school!" Maggie interposed hastily, in the same soothing voice as before. "And ... Elsie, is your mother waving to you?"

Elsie, looking up quickly, rose in a hurry.

"Yes, she is! Oh, I *hope* I haven't kept her waiting ... she does get so tired, not being able to move in the chair. ... Oh! *Oh!* OH!"

Her sudden scream was piercing; and the voices of Maggie and Joan rose to swell it. All three saw suddenly, with horror, that the insecurely-stationed bath-chair was moving of its own accord—perhaps the waving arm of Mrs. Maxwell had given it just the slight impetus that was needed. It was moving, quite smoothly, and faster and faster, towards the unguarded edge of the parade. Someone snatched at the handle behind, and just missed it. Elsie was running madly, screaming as she ran; but one does not make quick progress over shingle, and in any case she was many yards off. People were staring, running, shouting, and quite powerless to help in any way. The bath-chair glided smoothly and easily over the treacherous edge, and crashed horribly on the shingle, many feet below.

CHAPTER XIII

Forty Years On

JOAN had started with an unpleasant violence at the sudden, unexpected noise. She found herself sitting bolt upright. She heard herself crying out, in a strange voice: "Come in!" ... And quite suddenly, with a still more violent shock, she realised that she was in bed, and that the noise had been nothing worse than a knocking at her door.

"Miss Crewe asks me to say, Miss Partridge, that she is bringing the doctor to see you in five minutes."

The door closed again. But Joan remained sitting bolt upright, not moving, just staring in a slow, dazed way at one thing after another.

She was not, as she had supposed, sitting on Slonsea beach with Maggie Corrie. She was in bed; and the bedroom was her own familiar little room at St. Aldate's. Her arms, lying on the sheet in front of her, were clad in blue striped pyjama-sleeves. At the foot of the bed she could see her own familiar clothes— clothes of the nineteen-thirties—lying neatly folded, with blouse and drill-slip tidily disposed over the chair-back. And it was not evening. It was morning, and rather late morning at that; for the sunlight was very much farther round her wall than it usually was when the getting-up bell rang.

There were footsteps outside, and a hand on the handle; and Miss Crewe, ushering in the school doctor, looked immediately at Joan's head. ... Horrors! She ought, of course, to have taken advantage of the timely warning to get up and brush her hair, and make herself generally neat for inspection. But she felt thoroughly dull and stupefied, and she had a horrid idea that she looked so, too; and her voice, answering the usual

questions that doctors so dearly love to ask, sounded dazed
and queer. She said Ninety-Nine, and put out her tongue, and
performed all the ordinary tricks. And apparently the doctor
found her quite uninteresting, for he very soon prepared to go
with great briskness.

"Well, you haven't got measles, at any rate, young woman!"
he said; and went off with Miss Crewe to inspect somebody
else who had, and whose crop of spots was really worth a
doctor's notice.

Joan went on sitting up in bed, staring. And presently Miss
Crewe came back.

"Well, Joan, you seemed so much under the weather last
night, that I thought the doctor had better have a look at you,
as he was coming in any case. I am sure you're as glad as I am
to hear that it isn't measles."

"Yes, Miss Crewe."

"He thinks that you may as well go away to-day, instead of
waiting for to-morrow. You've lost half the morning already,
and it's hardly worth while to get up and go into school for
one afternoon."

"Go away?" Joan repeated nervously.

Her eyes were growing round with fright.

"Only till Monday, of course, like everybody else," said
Miss Crewe, hastening to reassure her—for the very odd girl
really looked so unusually odd. Did she suspect herself of
having some terrible unnamed disease? If she had expected
to be expelled, she couldn't have seemed more terrified! And,
apparently, she was not at all reassured, even now.

"Where … where am I going?" she gasped.

"To my aunt, Mrs. Corrie, at Slonsea, of course—don't you
remember? I have just rung her up; and luckily she can have
you to-day instead of to-morrow."

(Really, the girl was very queer! She now looked completely
panic-stricken, and she caught at Miss Crewe's hand.)

"Oh, please, *please*, no! Not there! Oh, *please* not!"

"Really, Joan, this is most extraordinary of you!" said Miss Crewe, in a voice that was far from gratified. "You seemed to like the idea yesterday; and nothing can have happened since then to make you change your mind."

(Oh, *couldn't* it! Even Headmistresses don't know everything.)

"I'd rather stay here," Joan murmured faintly.

"Certainly not!" said Miss Crewe. "You would be very much in the way, and it would be most rude to my aunt. The whole question is *settled*, Joan, and there is no more to say about it. I will send you up something to eat while you dress; and Mademoiselle will see you off by the two-fifteen."

She walked statelily out of the room; and Joan sat staring after her, her eyes filled with terror and despair.

She was sufficiently herself by this time, to realise that her adventure had been nothing but a dream; but she felt a mad conviction that it was the sort of dream which, however unlikely, comes true. She would be seen off; she would travel with odd-looking strangers; she would arrive at Slonsea, to find herself once more, and this time in reality, back in the eighteen-nineties—and she couldn't bear it! How unspeakably awful to go back, knowing this time what she was in for, to those clothes, that restricted life! She looked down at her pyjamas, and she stared round her room: electric light, running water, open window, comfortable drill-slip—she slowly counted them all. She heard a bell ring, and the voices of happy modern girls downstairs. … She gave a great jump where she sat, and cried: "Come in!"

"Miss Crewe asks me to say, Miss, that you must eat your lunch quickly, for the taxi will be here at ten to two."

Joan didn't make any answer, good or bad. She merely sat staring in silence at the tray that was placed by her side; and Gladys the housemaid retired with a flounce, to express freely downstairs her confirmed opinion of *that* Partridge girl, who couldn't say so much as Thank you. Just sat there looking nohow, she had, as if she was half-witted!

Joan, meanwhile, sat choking down a strictly limited amount of shepherd's pie; and then she got up and dressed, consuming at intervals a still more limited amount of prunes and custard. Nothing could save her. It was no use hoping for an earthquake, or anything drastic of that sort, because it wouldn't happen. So she packed her suit-case in a dull torpor of misery; and she put on, with a lingering affection, the easy undergarments about which she had never thought twice before, and her best stockings, and her beloved lizard shoes, and the pretty blue short-sleeved marocain that had been new for Easter Sunday. How very, very nice they all were, and how odd that she had never appreciated them before! Her wrist-watch was marking the quarter, as she pulled the Zip fastening of her case and prepared to go downstairs. ... What a jolly little room it was! And what a perfect idiot she had been to spend all this term grousing, because she hadn't been given a west one, across the passage.

Mademoiselle was, of course, fussing frantically in the hall, with a firm conviction that they would lose the train if they didn't start five minutes earlier than had been arranged—she was like that. But Joan didn't argue the point, or talk about anything at all. She got into the taxi and stared out, just looking at things—as if, Mademoiselle reflected with annoyance, she had never seen them before: which was, of course, only one of Joan's unlovely tricks, to save herself the trouble of talking. She did not realise—why should she?—that the silent girl beside her was feeling rather as a person on her way to the guillotine might have felt, taking her last look at the beloved streets of Paris.

She was understanding, for the first time and very keenly, the value of all these everyday commonplaces. The taxi in itself, for instance—how quick, how smoothly-running, how convenient! All the girls and women in the streets looked so cool and comfortable in their light and scanty clothes: for the day was hot. There was the Cinema, where St. Aldate's had gone in force last week to see the great Arctic film, so perfectly marvellous and enthralling. There were some of the town Guides, obviously off for some jolly expedition on this Early Closing day. ... There, in fact, was one long, rapid succession of things that belonged to the nineteen-thirties, and hadn't been so much as dreamed of, forty years ago.

"Tu as mal, Jo-an? Tu ne dis pas un mot!" cried Mademoiselle: a chatty person, without dignity.

Joan replied woodenly that she was "tout droit, merci." She knew better than that, of course; but her head was stupid with misery, and Mademoiselle's answering cries of anguish fell upon almost deaf ears. She had just seen something that gave her a sudden jolt, and hurt unbearably—the local Hospital. ... In some horrid unknown fever-hospital, as she had incredibly forgotten until this moment, kitchenmaid Grace was lying ill and miserable: pleasant, friendly Grace, who had always had a smile for Miss Joan, on the rare occasions when they met. And even that was not the worst—nothing like the worst. Mummy herself might take the infection: might be very ill: might *die*. Joan might never see her again. ...

She wouldn't see her again in any case, of course. She was going back to eighteen-ninety. ...

"Will you remain then in the taxi?" Mademoiselle inquired pungently; and Joan gave a great start, realising that they were at the station; and got out, and followed in a docile manner— she was so very near her guillotine! Mademoiselle took Joan's ticket, and dropped it, and thanked effusively, in her best English (which wasn't anything to boast of), a Boy Scout who picked it up for her, thus presumably doing his good deed for the day. And mercifully the train was in; and Mademoiselle conscientiously chose suitable company for Joan, and saw her

established, and stood ejaculating outside the carriage for ever
and ever and ever. . . .

They were off. Mademoiselle, her parting smile working
every muscle of her face, slipped slowly out of sight. . . . Joan,
who was not fond of languages, felt a sharp pang of regret
to think that she would never hear that high-pitched foreign
voice again.

It cost her a sensible effort to lift her eyes and look at her
fellow-passengers—she was so much afraid of what she might
see. But at least, this time, she had her beloved Zip suit-case
held tight upon her knee, having refused all offers of putting
it in the rack or under the seat. This time she would, at least,
reach her journey's end with a suitable change of raiment about
her. . . . She looked opposite, and saw a pleasant-looking elderly
lady, stout and comfortable and very badly dressed, reading a
book. She looked along the seat, and saw a very small Scots
boy in a kilt; and opposite him was an old clergyman reading a
paper, his collar hidden by an impressive beard. No likelihood,
thank heaven! of being pestered with conversation. She sat
and thought about school, and the many pleasant things in
school-life that she seemed never before to have appreciated
in the least at their proper value—the games, the clothes, the
freedom. It wasn't advisable to go on and think about home,
for that was quite unbearable. She turned her face to the
window, apparently giving her whole attention to the view; and
when at last the train stopped, and cries of "Slonsea! Slonsea!"
arose outside, she stood up with a start and a bewildered
glance round, almost as if she had been asleep. Clutching her
suit-case and her umbrella in hands that were suddenly very
cold, she stepped down out of the carriage.

There was a mist before her eyes, so that she couldn't see
properly. It would be better to wait for a minute or two, in
case, this time, Maggie had succeeded in coming to meet her;
but in any case it wouldn't matter—she had a perfectly clear

remembrance of the way out of the station and down to the Square. ...

"Is this Joan Partridge?"

Joan looked up, with a madly-beating heart, at the tall, smiling person who was speaking to her. The sense of bewilderment, instead of clearing, thickened. She heard herself gasping out something that seemed perfectly mad—and yet those kind eyes were quite familiar to her.

"Why—it's *Maggie!*"

The tall lady laughed out loud: though she, too, seemed rather bewildered.

"I can't imagine how you know me, since I haven't been photographed for twenty years! But you're quite right. I *am* Mrs. Corrie, and my name *is* Maggie!"

CHAPTER XIV

Betwixt and Between

NOTHING on earth would induce Joan to give up her green Zip suit-case to anyone—it was not heavy, and, *please*, she would rather carry it herself. So, the case being indeed light enough and the distance small, Mrs. Corrie gave her her own way: looking at her occasionally, as they walked, in rather an odd and considering manner. She had been warned to expect a girl who wasn't easy to handle; and, having a wide experience of girls, she had made no objection. But there was something here, she felt at once, that was quite unusual. This girl looked nothing more or less than *frightened*; and the tenacious clinging to her suit-case was part of the fright.

As they walked, she was looking about her cautiously, tentatively, as if expecting to see things that she feared and hated; and, as she looked, her eyes were slowly widening with incredulous surprise that was almost relief. What was there in the sight of an ordinary bicycle-shop to give her such satisfaction? and why should the outside of a Cinema make her look so gratified? Mrs. Corrie, who wasn't fond of the Pictures, hoped that this was not a young film-fan, who would expect to go to them every evening.

More than this—what could have been the reason of her extraordinary greeting? It wouldn't have been in the least like Miss Crewe (whose treatment of her girls was on the stiff side) to refer to her aunt as just "Maggie"—a thing she never dreamed of doing to Mrs. Corrie herself! And, apart from that, what had made this odd girl appear to recognise her hostess at sight, almost as if she had been an old friend? Mrs. Corrie puzzled her head in vain, and gave it up as a bad job.

Joan, for her part, was feeling stunned.

Since one South Coast watering-place is very like another, Slonsea was much as she had expected it to be: the unmathematically long Square leading to the usual Parade, with the usual shingle-beach and flat sea beyond. So far, this brief walk was almost exactly like that other dream-walk; and Mrs. Corrie's house, with steps leading up to it, corresponded well enough with what Joan had expected to see. But Mrs. Corrie herself—though in some mysterious way she was the Maggie of the dream—was dressed as the nineteen-thirties dress, and so were all the people whom they met. The traffic was the sort of motor-traffic to which Joan was accustomed. Girls in drill-slips were cycling home from school. Elder girls, and women old enough to know better, were plastered with lipstick and powder, and had thinned their unfortunate eyebrows to a Chinese pencil-line of unalterable surprise.

"I've stupidly forgotten my latch-key!" said Mrs. Corrie; and laughed, and rang an electric bell. They were admitted by a smart modern maid in a dark-green uniform; and Joan, glancing at the pillar-box at the corner, wondered what *she* would say if she were expected to ask permission, every time she wanted to run out and post a letter! The inside of the house was much the same, but the furniture was quite different: except for a large oil-painting hanging on the wall.

"That is my mother," said Mrs. Corrie.

"Yes," said Joan. "I know." And she did, indeed, know very well the old-fashioned cap and dress and figure. Those grey eyes, looking straight out at her, were the eyes that had been so scandalised by her drill-slip. The very firm mouth was the same that had insisted on shut windows, to keep out the dangerous night-air.

(" Now, what," thought Mrs. Corrie, "can that tone mean? Lucy Crewe may have shown her a photograph; and of course that sort of picture, hanging in my house, is likely to be my mother. But the child looks and speaks as if they had actually known each other—and she can't possibly have been born till after Mother's death!")

Aloud, she said:

"I expect you will like to take your hat off. I'll show you your room."

It was the same room, looking on to the Square, that Joan had occupied in her dream: but not at all the same furniture. Everything was pleasant and ordinary in the modern way, with a shelf of interesting-looking books, a little writing-table, and a comfortable basket-chair. Yet the sense of her dream was so strong upon her that, when left alone, she could hardly bear to leave her Zip case behind her, lest she should find it gone when she returned. She went downstairs looking dazed; and Mrs. Corrie was freshly puzzled.

"Have you ever been to Slonsea before?" she asked, pouring out tea in the pleasant drawing-room.

(What an *extraordinary* girl! Even that most simple and obvious question made her start, and turn a little pale, and stammer out an unintelligible answer that seemed to be first Yes and then No. Mrs. Corrie really felt that it was hardly fair of Lucy to have sent her, without warning, a girl who wasn't quite right in her head.)

"I had asked a friend to supper this evening, before I knew that you were coming a day early," she said conversationally. "Now I've asked her to bring her girl, who is about your age."

"Thank you very much. What is her name?" Joan asked, still in the same tone; and, on being told "Rachel Toft," looked oddly—relieved, Mrs. Corrie would have thought, if it hadn't been absurd. She inquired if Joan had any friends in the place; and again received the most curious, garbled answer. She … she thought so—no, she *didn't* think so! … Mrs. Corrie, quite disturbed, thought she had never met such a queer girl. It was not only the things she said: it was her puzzled, dazed, bewildered look. The kindest thing seemed to be, to ask no more questions, only ply her with food: which, mercifully, she ate with a good appetite.

"Shall we go out?" Mrs. Corrie suggested, after tea; and was struck again by the extraordinary expression of relief on Joan's face, as she came down with her hat on. The cause of it would have been more puzzling still; for it was merely that the green Zip suit-case was still where it had been left, and hadn't been spirited away, or changed into something different.

"Must I—must I wear gloves?"

"Gloves, on a hot evening like this!" laughed Mrs. Corrie. (And the odd girl looked relieved again. *What* was she afraid of? What did she expect or dread?)

Joan found the Parade exactly what she had expected to find it: hot, glaring, soulless, and crowded, exactly as she remembered it. As she had walked there with Maggie Corrie before, so she walked with Maggie Corrie now—only this Maggie knew nothing about that other walk. Her voice was so exactly as Joan remembered it, that it kept giving her shocks of frightened reminiscence; and then she would look up quickly, and get a fresh shock from seeing the same kind eyes, set in the face of an oldish woman dressed in modern clothes. The likeness and the difference, all mixed and jumbled together, made Joan's head spin, so that she heard herself answering vaguely and strangely.

If she did not look at her companion, she could steady herself by seeing that the traffic and the passers-by were of her own time. And presently they took a motor-bus (mentally very steadying, whatever it might be considered physically: for there weren't, there *weren't* any in Victorian days!) and went up to the old Castle, perched high and secure on its cliff. And, as Joan had never been there before, she recovered, and felt almost her natural self again—and Mrs. Corrie began to revise her opinion. There was nothing odd about the girl, after all. She proved pleasant and intelligent, and they talked very comfortably together.

Joan found her bewilderment lessening a little. It seemed that Mrs. Corrie was still Maggie Corrie—a puzzling thing in itself—because she had married a distant cousin who had been killed in the Great War. From the very little that she said, Joan gathered that she had been widowed after only a month or two, and that she had never had a home of her own, but had just gone on living with her mother at the house in the Square. When Mrs. Corrie went on quickly to talk of her own school days, and of the difference between Then and Now, she found Joan incredibly sympathetic and understanding; and they left the Castle, and got into another bus, on the best of terms.

"There are the Baths," said Mrs. Corrie. "Did you bring your bathing-dress? I thought you might like to go there with Rachel Toft, to-morrow afternoon—I have arranged some tennis for Saturday."

Now, what was there in that pleasant plan to make this girl—suddenly an odd girl again—turn silent, and even a little pale? Her look across the road had something like aversion in it—and yet she said she was a good swimmer and liked it! and there couldn't, surely, be anything in her mind against these particular Baths, well known to be some of the best on the South Coast. Mrs. Corrie, a native of Slonsea and proud of it, felt a little annoyed. She dropped the subject; and the rest of their short journey was silent.

The Zip case was safely in its place, with all Joan's things inside it; and she changed, and came down to find that Mrs. Toft and Rachel had arrived, and were pleasant and friendly people. Mrs. Toft, it seemed, had been an old school-fellow of Mrs. Corrie's; and Joan, gazing at her, wondered if she had met her before during that dream-visit. She was tall and cheerful, with a flow of amusing conversation; and she was extremely well dressed. When Mrs. Corrie addressed her as Ella, Joan couldn't keep back a start of excitement—for surely this must be Ella Tybald the Awful, of whom she had heard so much! They were laughing over old school recollections; and Mrs. Toft, turning to Joan in her lively way, said:

"You know, I was a very bad girl in those days! and Mrs. Corrie didn't like me at all."

"Yes," said Joan. "I know!"

It had slipped out before she could stop herself; and she felt herself turning cold with horror. An astonished pause followed, as well it might: broken by Mrs. Toft's saying, with a laugh:

"Why, have you been telling tales out of school, Maggie?"

She sounded far from pleased; and Mrs. Corrie, too, was obviously upset—surprised, and annoyed, and distressed. She said, with considerable emphasis:

"No, indeed, Ella! I have told Joan a good deal about the old school; but I am quite sure that I never mentioned your name at all."

"She must be a clairvoyante, then!" said Mrs. Toft, passing it off with another laugh. "Or is it that I *still* look such a bad character, Joan?"

What an awful and unexplainable situation! Poor Joan mumbled a hasty denial. She stared at her plate, feeling herself growing redder and redder; and they were merciful, and talked of something else. Mrs. Toft, it seemed, had been spending the afternoon with another old schoolfellow, who was a complete invalid: almost always in pain, hardly ever able to leave her sofa.

"Did she have an accident?" Joan inquired, rather faintly—but anything was better than to sit in silence, thinking about her dreadful *faux pas*.

"Oh, no!" said Mrs. Toft. "The foolish fashions of our young days had a good many victims; and she was one of the most foolish, and is suffering for it now. You girls will never be able to imagine what some of us went through to get down to a nineteen-inch waist—though we never starved ourselves as some of you do."

As she spoke, she looked at Joan, surprised and puzzled as Mrs. Corrie had been. The girl looked so—understanding: almost as if she had some personal acquaintance with those long-ago days and their follies. A very odd girl! ... She could not know, of course, that Joan firmly believed the invalid old-girl to be one of the Derwents, and had only just prevented herself from saying so, and asking which.

They played Hearts, a cheerful if irritating game; and the evening passed quickly and pleasantly. It was surprisingly late, when Mrs. Toft at last said firmly that she must go.

"Rachel isn't so lucky as you," she said to Joan. "*She* has school to-morrow morning."

"I was wondering," said Mrs. Corrie, "if Rachel could spare time to go with Joan to the Baths, to-morrow afternoon?" And Rachel, a cheerful person of great energy, like her mother, said: "Yes, rather!" with enthusiasm. But Mrs. Corrie, looking at Joan, saw once more that queer expression that she couldn't understand.

"You said you *did* like swimming, Joan?"

The only possible answer, of course, was to say Yes with all the enthusiasm that could be mustered; but it wasn't a great success. Mrs. Toft, at the hall door, murmured that that seemed rather an odd girl, didn't it? and was answered with an embarrassment that spoke volumes.

"Don't let her victimise you, Maggie!" she exhorted severely. "You know your besetting sin—you're far too kind to everyone!" And she went down the steps with Rachel.

Mrs. Corrie, coming back from seeing them off, found Joan standing in the drawing-room looking—odd. There was no other word for it: a mixture of anxiety, and nervousness, and dread. At the suggestion of bed, she even turned a little pale. But she said good-night normally, and went upstairs without protest—and, indeed, what could there have been for her to protest about? Mrs. Corrie, a little relieved, went back into the drawing-room, and took up a book which interested her very much. It had been sent her by Miss Crewe the day before, and she had only had time to begin it.

Upstairs, Joan switched on her bedroom light with trembling fingers—relieved, though, that it still *was* electric light—and looked round nervously. There, still safe and unaltered, was the green Zip case; and her own familiar pyjamas were laid out on the bed, and everything in the room was present-day and not Victorian. *But*—it was in this very room that she had gone to sleep, and awakened to find everything changed. Oh, was that going to happen again? If it did, she couldn't possibly bear it.

She went and stood by the wide-open window, and stared out; and, as it happened, she couldn't have done a more inadvisable thing. For, in this half-light, what she saw might have been of any period—the unchanging sea, the parade with its distant figures passing dimly along, a distant lighthouse sending out revolving lights. Even people on the pavement underneath were indistinct in the dusk of the summer night, and their clothes might have been any sort of clothes. In two minutes, Joan did not know if she was looking out at Slonsea of the nineteen-thirties, or Slonsea of forty years ago. A dreadful terror took possession of her. Her hands grew cold and damp, and her heart beat so that it nearly stifled her. Lines learned and recited at school began to drum in her ears.

> "… in fear and dread,
>   And, having once looked round, goes on
>   And turns no more his head,
>   Because he knows some frightful thing …"

"My dear Joan, what a scream!" said the voice of Mrs. Corrie behind her. "Didn't you hear me knock?"

Joan gasped, and shook her head dumbly.

"You know why I have come, I'm sure!"

"You've come ... you've come to say that I must shut the window. ..."

"On a hot night like this? Hardly! I saw your light, when I went out to post a letter; and I came to see why you were not yet in bed."

"I can't ... I can't ..."

"Can't go to bed! Why not?" asked Mrs. Corrie, in justifiable surprise. And again she felt that Lucy Crewe really had no business to saddle her with a girl of such extreme peculiarities.

Joan swallowed once or twice, quite audibly. Her answer, when it came, was fainter than ever.

"I ... I'm frightened ..."

"*Frightened?* Of what? And why won't you turn and look at me?"

It seemed to Joan, now thoroughly worked up, that that was, of all things, the most impossible to do. As long as she went on looking out of the window at the quickly-dimming prospect, she didn't *know* that anything was altered. But one glance behind her might show the room that she remembered so vividly—the curtained bed, the muslin-draped dressing-table, the long-sleeved nightdress laid out for her to wear. She clung frantically, with both hands, to the window-sill.

"I can't, I *can't* go back to the eighteen-nineties!" she sobbed frantically.

CHAPTER XV

The Late Joan Grouse

MRS. CORRIE did not answer for a moment; perhaps she was too much astonished. When she spoke, her voice was incisive and not particularly gentle: for there are times when it is no kindness to be too kind.

"That is a good thing—since you could not possibly do it, if you did want to."

Joan wrenched herself round, staring with wide, terrified eyes. Better, after all, to know the worst than to go on dreading it! ... She saw an uncurtained bed, an undraped dressing-table, a green Zip case, and a pair of blue-striped pyjamas, lying on the bed. Standing by the door was not Maggie Corrie the Victorian girl, but the elderly Mrs. Corrie of to-day. The light that revealed all this was an electric light. Outside, something hooted noisily by, that could be nothing but a motor-bicycle. ... Joan suddenly found tears running fast down her face.

"My dear child," said Mrs. Corrie, in an entirely new voice that was very kind, "do tell me what on *earth* is the matter with you!"

And Joan told: with sobs and tears, sitting on the bed beside her pyjamas, with Mrs. Corrie on the other side, holding her hand in a comforting clasp. She told how this was (or was not) her first visit to Slonsea. She told how she had (or had not) known Mrs. Corrie as the girl Maggie, and Maggie's mother as a very different Mrs. Corrie. She told, in a jumbled confusion, of long-skirted tennis, of clinging, voluminous bathing-dresses, of wasp-waists, of high-perched sailor-hats, held precariously in place by black elastic. She told of closed windows and red baize sausages to keep out draughts; and of a lady wearing a respirator; and of many other things. It says much for Mrs. Corrie's brains and patience that, after listening attentively for many minutes, she did at last disentangle the main purport of all this.

"Well, Joan," she said at last, in a comforting and bracing voice, when at last there came a break in the torrent of revelation, "you have had a most remarkable and interesting dream; but it *was* a dream, you know."

"You're quite sure?" Joan panted, casting a hunted look round. (But it was still all right.)

"Absolutely and positively certain!" said Mrs. Corrie. "And I am most thankful that you have at last brought yourself to tell me all this—for I was really beginning to wonder if you were out of your mind!"

"I'm not, am I?" cried Joan, freshly startled.

"Certainly not!" said Mrs. Corrie again, with a most reassuring laugh. "If I had still thought so, it would have been the very last thing that I should have said, you know. I think that, somehow, you have learnt a rather wonderful amount about forty years ago; and that you were upset about things generally, and so in a likely condition for dreaming; and that you have a very vivid imagination! How *did* you learn all these details, Joan? Did Miss Crewe show you, by any chance, a very old photograph of my mother and me? She *did!* Well, that accounts for something, then. But all those details. ...."

A light broke out suddenly on her face. She left the room quickly; and returned with a book in her hand.

"Have you by any chance read this?" she asked, holding it up.

In all these hectic happenings, Joan had altogether forgotten how she had read "Our Mothers," ages and ages ago, in Miss Crewe's drawing-room; but she knew the book again at once.

"Why, of course! I read a lot of it, while I was waiting for Miss Crewe. ..."

"She sent it to me yesterday," said Mrs. Corrie. "Look at some of the pictures."

She turned over pages, pointing to this and that; and Joan saw in a flash where she had learnt all that surprising knowledge of Victorian days. There were the sailor-hats, the bustled skirts, the bathing-dresses—even the stays! Not all the stuff of which her dream was made had come, of course, from that interesting volume; for she had listened to plenty of auntish people telling her how lucky she and her contemporaries were to have, or not to have, the disadvantages or advantages unknown to a generation ago. The whole thing had been churned up in her dreaming brain, producing what, even now, she did not like to remember.

"You don't want to go back to my early days, do you?" said Mrs. Corrie, seeing this; and her laugh had a sigh in it. "But there was something to be said for them, after all, Joan. You don't believe that, do you? No, of course you don't! But *we* weren't deafened with traffic noises, and we didn't have thousands of people killed on the roads every year. We hadn't so many amusements as you; but we were very much more contented with what we had. Books were much dearer, and we had not nearly so many; but we read those we had over and over, until we really knew them, and loved them. We didn't cycle, and we had no cars, and very few of us had carriages; but you modern girls don't know how jolly it is to walk and talk, day after day, with your particular friend. Our visitors didn't dash down to us for a week-end; they came expecting to stay for a fortnight, and they settled down into our home-life, and we missed them terribly when they went. Games *were* games in my day, not organised sports; and the people who couldn't play like professionals had a chance to enjoy themselves. ... Of course you have some things that we should have loved: Guides—and Woolworth—and getting to know most of England in your cars, instead of only the little bit near where we or our friends lived. But, taken all round, I wouldn't change my girlhood for yours, Joan, for *anything!* I don't envy you your wireless. I hate it; and the Pictures give me a headache. And— *we* had pockets! In fact, I still have."

With a laugh that was a real laugh, she turned out a collection that a schoolboy might have respected: a handkerchief, a penknife, a pencil, a half-dried potato—"for rheumatism," she explained, seeing Joan stare: "and an excellent thing, too, though my doctor snorts at it"—a thimble, a little bunch of keys, and a shoe-button.

"My dressmaker is horrified! She says stiffly: 'I suppose you must have your old-fashioned pocket?'—but I am very firm with her. And the result is, that I'm not always losing a silly little bag, or getting it snatched from me in the street. ... *Joan*, look at the clock! You will be worn out, and fit for nothing to-morrow. Get into bed at once!"

In spite of all explanations and assurances: in spite of Zip case and pyjamas, all present and in order: Joan felt one last momentary qualm at the idea of falling asleep in this room, that she knew so painfully well. And Mrs. Corrie was very quick of apprehension.

"My dear, you aren't *still* afraid that your dream will come true?"

"Not—not really!" said Joan, very much ashamed.

"Were my times so dreadful to you, then?"

Joan rushed out the truth in a burst.

"It wasn't that! It was ... Mother!"

Mrs. Corrie, being so quick, saw at once all that lay behind that rather shaky word. She realised what an appalling thing it must have been to find oneself divided, by more than forty years, from one's own home and people. And she behaved as very few grown-ups would have had the sense to do—yes, though the clock on the mantelpiece was telling an incredible tale.

"Sit down at once, you poor child, and write to your mother, and tell her everything—and never mind the time! If you are feeling like that, you'll never sleep till you have done it. You'll find all you want on the table … Good-night, my dear!"

She was gone, with a kind, quick smile from the door. And Joan sat down, and wrote and wrote—deeply comforted, at the very outset, by finding stamps with King George's head upon them—and staggered confusedly into bed, unable to keep her eyes open for another minute, as the clock reproachfully struck One. It hadn't been at all the sort of letter that she had meant to write. It hadn't been like any previous letter that she had ever written to her mother, or to anyone else. Though she had started out to tell her incredible adventures, after the first page there was hardly anything at all about herself; but there was a great deal about the trouble and worry that poor darling Mummy must have had, and was she *quite* sure that she was all right? And oh, she *must* be careful! And how was poor Grace? And would Mummy please, if she had time, get a *large* bunch of *black* grapes (heavily underlined), and send it to Grace's hospital with a note to say how sorry Joan was for her? and would she subsequently stop the price of the said grapes out of the said Joan's pocket-money? It was, of course, *horrid* (again heavily underlined) not to come home for half-term; but there was no occasion to worry, as Joan was safe at Slonsea, and was quite sure that she was going to have a most topping time (as far as was compatible with being away from home), for Mrs. Corrie was most awfully nice and kind. Joan was going to the Baths to-morrow with a terribly nice girl who had come to supper that evening; she was going to play tennis on Saturday, which would also be terribly nice. Wasn't it topping of Miss Crewe to give her an extra day? But that didn't mean that she was anything but quite, *absolutely* well. …

A rending yawn pulled the writer up at that point, and she

looked round the room for a final reassurance; and her Zip case, and her pyjamas, and the wide-open window, and the delicious sound of a motor-lorry back-firing outside, all combined to give her a heavenly feeling of comfort. And then her eyes fell amazedly on the clock, and she realised guiltily that she hadn't been writing the truth. It wasn't that evening that Rachel and her mother had come to supper: it was yesterday. And it wasn't to-morrow that she was going ...

Realising all this, she suddenly realised something else as well: that her eyes were closing as she sat, and that her letter had better be fastened up at once, before she fell asleep on it. And so it was, and the address was written, between immense yawns, in a horribly scrawling and untidy manner that would have shocked Miss Crewe to the very soul. But possibly Mrs. Partridge, when she received it that evening, found it all that she could have wished.

The Fifth Form at St. Aldate's were discussing their past half-term holiday: only just past, with that irritating swiftness which is the great fault of holidays. Peggy Mills had heard more of her Constantinople prospects, and was more full of them than ever. Alison Hughes told, with vast amusement, how seven of them had set off for a caravanning week-end in a caravan warranted to hold four; and how they had broken down seven miles from anywhere, with only a pound of ginger-nuts and three packets of chocolate between them, and nothing to drink at all, and what *topping* fun it had all been! Philippa Minchin, listening in a pale horror, told how she and her mother had been to a large and fashionable hotel in a large and fashionable watering-place, and what a pity it was that the Duke and Duchess of Frogmore had left just before. ...

"Philippa, you are the last word in snobs!" Audrey crushed her to the earth; and then looked round. "Oh, help! Here comes Joan Grouse!"

The little group fell into that curious silence that was only too apt to greet Joan. Even the kind Katharine spoke in rather a constrained voice.

"Well, Joan—had a good time?"

"*Topping!*" said Joan; and, looking happily round, she wondered why they all seemed so surprised by her answer. Was it such an odd thing to enjoy a holiday? How comfortable and cool they all appeared, sitting about on that hot day with their bare arms, and short skirts, and hatless, shingled heads! She hadn't yet got over enjoying the comfort of all these things. She hadn't yet forgotten what it meant to wear clumsy, ankle-long frocks, and stiff, tight stays, and a hat fastened on with elastic. The screech of a most offensive motor-horn outside was music in her ears.

"What did you do?" Audrey inquired curiously.

Joan told them: not making a song about it, for after all there wasn't so very much to tell. She had been staying with Miss Crewe's fearfully nice aunt at that jolly place Slonsea, and she had played tennis with some ripping girls, and the Baths were *topping*. And what had everyone else been doing?

Listening, more or less, to an endless babble from Peggy about Constantinople, Joan kept her hand tight on a letter which (no longer, unfortunately, having a pocket) she had tucked down the front of her dress. She had found it waiting for her; and it told how Mummy was perfectly all right, and quarantine was nearly over, and no one in the house showed any suspicious symptom, and Grace was getting on as well as possible. No letter, in fact, could have been more completely satisfactory.

"Hullo—what is it?" Audrey called to a servant, coming out from the house. "Peggy, you're making such a din that I can't hear a word she says!"

She got up—not sorry, perhaps, to get away from Constantinople—and took the message, and called back.

"Joan, you're wanted—Joan *Partridge!*"

Joan got up, full of surprise and gratification. It was the first time, for many terms, that Audrey had ever called her by her proper name.

Books to Treasure

Old favourites

E M CHANNON:
Expelled from School
Her Second Chance

BESSIE MARCHANT:
The Two New Girls (eBook only)

DOROTHEA MOORE:
A Runaway Princess (eBook only)
Brenda of Beech House (eBook only)
Fen's First Term (eBook only)
Septima Schoolgirl (eBook only)
Wanted: an English Girl

EVELYN SMITH:
Queen Anne series
Seven Sisters at Queen Anne's
Septima at School
Phyllida in Form III

The First Fifth Form
The Small Sixth Form
Biddy and Quilla

eBooks available for download from all Amazon sites
sales@bookdragonbooks.co.uk   www.bookdragonbooks.co.uk

Lightning Source UK Ltd.
Milton Keynes UK
UKOW06f1709170315

248046UK00001B/31/P